POST MORTEM AT PADUA

An Oxford Key Mystery

LYNN MORRISON

The Marketing Chair

Cover design by Emilie Yane Lopes

Published by

The Marketing Chair Press, Oxford, England

LynnMorrisonWriter.com

Paperback ISBN: 978-1-8380391-7-2

Contents

Chapter One

What would it be like to have the most famous minds from ancient Rome whispering advice in your ear? That's the question running through my mind as I take in the greenish colour of the large pool before me.

The stagnant, murky water does little to tempt me into taking a dip. That's probably for the best, given we're in a museum and swimming is definitely off limits. All around us, tourists wander past, speaking a myriad of languages as they ooh and ahh over the displays.

I glance at my friend Kate, giving her a look filled with trepidation. "The Roman baths? Are we really going to create a new connection to the magical field with all these visitors wandering past?"

Kate shrugs and purses her lips. "This wasn't my idea, remember? It was Mathilde who came up with the location. You have to admit, this place has a wealth of history attached to it. That bathing pool you're glaring at is over two thousand years old, Nat."

I take a step back to get a better look at our surroundings. Although the city of Bath is only an hour and a half from Oxford,

I haven't visited before. According to the brochure in my hand, this ancient building was once a centre for rest, beauty, and even worship for the Ancient Romans who ruled old Britannia.

Now, anyone who can afford the entrance ticket can go back in time and see how the Romans lived. Displays around the sprawling centre highlight the wondrous achievements, like the Roman plumbing, which still work today. There would be plenty to learn if only we could speak with the people who built the baths so many years ago.

If all goes well, we may soon find out.

Mathilde chooses that moment to join us, her face bright with excitement. "Look at this place!" she exclaims. "It's in incredible condition. I just know our attempt to make a magical connection will work this time."

Kate and I exchange sideways glances, neither of us sharing Mathilde's confidence. It's not that we have anything against making the attempt, nor against the location. It's simply that we've tried and failed enough times now that our enthusiasm for the challenge is waning.

Mathilde senses our hesitation and scores us both with a scorching glare. "We've got to have faith in ourselves. For all we know, belief and confidence play an important role in the success or failure of our attempts. Don't doom us before we have the chance to try!"

"You're right, Mathilde," I admit, much chagrinned. "Sorry for being such a downer. I promise, we want to make this work as much as you do. It's just hard to keep up the faith after our series of failures."

Mathilde wraps an arm over my shoulders and gives me a reassuring squeeze. "Look at H over there," she says, pointing further up the walkway. I follow her instructions until my gaze lands on a cat-sized, scaly black creature tucked in between a pair of tourists. As far as they're concerned, he's nothing more than a black and white cat wandering around the Roman bath. Only we three prefects can see his real identity.

"H spotted those animal statuettes as soon as we came through the doors. Think how ecstatic he would be if we could bring even one of them to life."

I can't stop the fond smile which crosses my face. H, full name Humphrey, has stuck by my side through thick and thin. Risking embarrassment in a crowd of strangers is the least I can do to show him how much I care about him.

When I spy a similar expression on Kate's face, I know we're up for the challenge. "Okay, I'm in. But before we start, let me check my notes." I flip my notebook open to the right page and skim over it. "None of our indoor locations have worked, so this time we're aiming for an outdoor space with a natural light source."

"Check," Mathilde answers, pointing to the bright beam of sunlight illuminating the far corner of the pool.

"Excellent," I tick the top item on my list and try not to think about the time we used a handheld torch. Forget forging a connection. We didn't even manage a flicker. "Next up is a location with a deep-rooted history?"

"You can tick that one twice," Kate replies. "Between the original Roman settlers who frequented the place and the Victorians who rediscovered it, the Baths have seen millennia of use."

So had all the other places we'd tried so far... but I keep that thought to myself. "Right then, the last item is the copper rods. Do we have enough to space them properly around the pool?"

Mathilde hefts the weighty pack from her back and sighs as she sets it on the ground. "I grabbed way more than what we estimated we'd need. I do not want to run short this time."

With no items left to tick off, I close my notebook and shove it into my bag. "Alright then, let's get to work."

I don't know whether it is the breathtaking setting or the thought of just how many people have visited the baths, but as I place the copper rods around the pool, my excitement builds.

Maybe Mathilde is right. So what if all our other attempts failed? We're smart women, brimming with courage and determination. We've solved murders and uncovered elaborate schemes. Why shouldn't this time be a success?

Together, our little group troops around the pool until we're standing in the sunlight. Kate retrieves a white cloth from her handbag and carefully unfolds the fabric to reveal a polished gold medallion.

"From the Ashmolean archives," she explains in a whisper. "It was discovered here among the ruins. Be careful with it, Mathilde. It should go without saying, but just in case... it's priceless."

Mathilde takes a deep breath and holds it in as she wraps her fingers around the medallion. Then she turns to the face the sun and lowers down until she's kneeling beside H. With great care, she shifts the medallion in the sunlight until it catches the sun. She exhales, finally, and as the last step in the process, manoeuvres the antique piece until the sunlight reflects off of it and onto the first copper rod in our series.

I can barely contain myself when the air over the pool shifts and swirls. As the haze clears, the green pool is instead a clear blue, and dark-haired women splash and float. Their voices, ever faint, prove to be speaking in Latin.

My head whips left and right as I take in the scene before us. The elaborately braided coiffures identify the women as among the wealthy. They bask in the warm pool, revelling in the bright sun and the healing touch of Bath's mineral waters.

"It's working!" Mathilde squeals. And then she groans when the scene flickers and disappears. She tries again, her hand shaking as she struggles to line up the ray of sunshine with the metallic surfaces.

H, sensing her desperation, lends a hand in the only way he can. He backs up a step and takes a running leap into the air. He drops like a cannonball into the tranquil waters, sending waves lapping up the side.

Once again, the view of Bath's Eternals returns. The ancient Roman women are all staring at the wyvern swimming beside them. Their shouts of confusion and concern fill the air one moment, and go silent the next.

No matter how much H splashes, and Mathilde shifts, the connection refuses to stick. After a few more seconds of trying, a cloud passes over the sun and brings our experiment to an abrupt end.

H swims over to where we are and climbs onto the side, water dripping from his wings. He shakes, sending water droplets spraying over us, and then finishes the drying process with a carefully directed flame from his snout.

Sensing that both H and Mathilde need a moment to collect themselves, Kate and I work in silence to collect the rods we'd placed with such hope.

When we're back at their side, I offer Mathilde a hand and pull her to her feet. "Come on, Mathilde. I'll treat you to a cup of tea and a scone in the museum cafe."

Mathilde, however, isn't ready to move on. She stares at the near-pristine remnants of Britain's ancient Roman civilisation, unable to believe that our plan didn't work. "We've followed the instructions perfectly, Nat. I don't understand why we continue to fail. I'm starting to think maybe we aren't capable of duplicating the original work. Or, at least, not on our own."

I hate to admit it, but she might be right. But that leaves us with a giant problem. If we can't figure out how to forge a new magical connection, who can?

Chapter Two

T he Senior Common Room door opens with a loud creak,
announcing my entrance better than any words could do.
Not that it matters. This late in the evening, there is no one here
to witness our return to St Margaret College.

My shoulders slumped, I trudge into the welcoming room,
turning a blind eye to the pale blue walls and creased newspapers
begging to be read. My friends follow fast on my heels, Mathilde
and Kate as downtrodden as I am. Even H is quiet, his wings
hanging so low that they nearly scrape the carpet.

"Should we raid the biscuit cupboard?" I ask. Mathilde nods
gratefully and H perks up. The chance to eat a sugary treat always
brightens his spirits.

By the time Harry arrives, we're sprawled across the sofas
munching on chocolate-covered digestive biscuits. As the
Executive Assistant to the Principal of St Margaret College,
Harry would be well within her rights to eject the lot of us from
the building, particularly given the hour. But as one of our nearest
and dearest friends, she does nothing of the sort. Instead, she lets
the door close behind her and leans a shoulder against the wall,
taking our measure. With her white pageboy haircut and trim

figure, she looks every inch the competent professional that she is.

I wish I could say the same for the rest of us. My polka dot dress hangs limply, showing signs of a long day spent travelling. Mathilde's hair, now growing out from her bob, is once again twisted up and held in place with a pencil. Somehow, Kate still looks polished and professional, but her scowl ruins the impact of her expensive ensemble.

"I take it your day wasn't a success," Harry states, not needing an answer. "What happened this time?"

"The same thing that happened the last three times we attempted to create a new connection to the magic," I grumble. "I don't understand what we could possibly be doing wrong. We've followed every instruction to the nth degree."

"Sir Christopher made it seem so simple when he handed over his notes and said it was up to us to decide where to take the magic next." Kate bemoans, her frustration evident. "There is obviously some step we're missing, or more to it than he realised."

"How can we miss a step when there are only two?" I ask, raising my voice as my annoyance gets the better of me. "First, he told us to find a location which has a deep historical significance. We've tried St Andrews College in Scotland, Canterbury Cathedral, Westminster Abbey, and now the Roman ruins in Bath. We've got the copper rods he designed and sourced artefacts connected to each site. Yet, we can't stabilise a connection to the magic for more than a few seconds."

"We shouldn't give up," Mathilde interjects, digging deep to find some positive spin. "Things worked differently in Sir Christopher's time. The scientific method didn't even exist. They learned through trial and error. We have to do the same. I'm sure that if we stick with it, we'll eventually create a new connection."

Sensing we need a distraction, Harry clears her throat and draws our attention. "Perhaps you prefects need a break. In fact, that's why I asked you to come here this evening. I have some news."

"Good news?" I ask, desperately hoping the answer is yes.

"Good news, indeed." Harry crosses the room to take a seat. She eyes the biscuit crumbs on my skirt and opts for the chair instead of joining me on the sofa. "The University and City of Oxford made a joint announcement today. They've signed a new twin city agreement with a university town in Italy."

Whatever I expected Harry to say, this isn't it. "That's interesting, but I don't see how it qualifies as good news."

"I'm getting to that," Harry says, shushing me. "There will be a formal ceremony held in three weeks' time in Italy. As St Margaret College is one of the sponsors of the project, I've been asked to go down early and work with our Italian counterparts at the event. And you, Natalie Payne, our very own Head of Ceremonies, have been assigned as well."

"Italy!" Mathilde gasps, taking the words right out of my mouth. "Which city? Is it Bologna? Or Rome? They both have well-known universities."

"You're on the right track," Harry replies. "We're going to Padua, or as the Italians call it, Padova. It's near Venice, in the northern part of the country."

"Padova?" Kate's scowl disappears. "Oh, Padova is lovely! Lavinia, one of my closest friends, lives there. Perhaps I can find an excuse to come along with you." Her voice trails off, her mind already putting together a plan.

"I wish I had an excuse to go to Padua," Mathilde mumbles, feeling left out. "I'd love to visit their anatomical theatre. It's the oldest in the world, and was purpose-built to allow students to watch as their professors conducted post mortem investigations." Mathilde stops when she catches sight of my expression. "Don't wrinkle your nose, Nat! Modern medicine owes its existence to those early studies of the human body."

"I've had enough of death in the past year to last me for a lifetime," I groan. "Can't you find an excuse to come along? I'll happily sacrifice my place on that macabre tour."

"I do have some annual leave to use up before the end of the year. I could put in a request for some time off... maybe a long weekend. But I'll be hard-pressed to get my request approved so quickly."

"You've got to ask, Mathilde. It could be a ladies' trip!" I feel a spark of excitement in my chest. "Do you think it would be safe for all of us to be gone for a week?"

"The magical field is stable now," Harry reminds us. "You ladies put a stop to that awful man who was trying to steal Oxford's magic. The Eternals have things well in hand. There's no reason you couldn't all three get away."

"There's one reason," a croaky voice pipes up. We all turn to look at the little, scaly black wyvern who is literally fuming. "You can't leave me 'ere all on my own!"

I reach down and give his head a gentle scratch. "What if you came with us, H?"

H chokes out a cloud of smoke, his surprise clear. "Come with you? Really?"

"Why not? You've got your medallion, which allows you to remain connected to the magical field, no matter where you are. You've been using it to come along with us on our trips around the UK. Why not take it a step further? You deserve a holibob as much as the rest of us."

"Maybe I'll meet another Eternal there. You think they might 'ave some creatures in Italy, Nat?" H asks, his eyes wide.

My heart breaks at the sight of his hopeful face. As defeated as Kate, Mathilde, and I feel, it has been even worse on H. At every place we've visited, he's wandered around, staring wistfully at grotesque gargoyles and animal statues. The creatures in Oxford have long since fallen into their own habits, leaving H with no one to call a close friend. Other than me, that is. But between my job, refurbishing my house, and planning my wedding, I've not had much time to spend with him.

"Oh, H! I'm sure Italy is filled with wonderful Eternals, but I don't see how we'd open a connection there given our repeated failures here in England." I wince as his expression falls. "For starters, we'd be missing a key component — how could we get our hands on a local artefact to use in the connection process?"

"I know someone we could ask," Kate offers, her voice hesitant. "But I have no idea how we would explain it to her."

I turn to Kate, caught off-guard by her statement. "Who?"

"Lavinia. My friend. She works for the university museum department, and has done so for at least the last decade. In fact, I suppose it's part of the reason I ended up here. She's always spoken positively about her job. Something of that must have stuck in my head, and encouraged me to apply when I heard about the opening at the Ashmolean." Kate chuckles. "Lavinia and I are a lot alike. We met while doing our post-graduate studies and hit it off. I shouldn't be surprised our careers ended up mirroring one another."

"There you go, missie," H chimes in. "We can ask the Italian Kate to lend us a 'and.'"

The Italian Kate? H's words spin around in my mind, sparking off a new train of thought. Could that be the piece we've been missing in our attempts to create a new magical connection?

I sit up straight, my breath catching. "Why didn't we think of this before?" I look at my friends, but Mathilde and Kate only stare back with a puzzled expression on their faces. "There aren't two steps to the process—there are three! First, we need the right location. Second, we need the physical materials, like the copper rods and the artefacts. Third, we need the people!" I smile, raising my eyebrows and nodding my head in encouragement as I wait for them to catch on.

Mathilde's eyebrows draw into a line as her eyes flick from side to side. "Nat, we've had people. The three of us. We're all prefects with a connection to the magic."

"No," I correct her. "We're prefects with a connection to *Oxford's* magic. When Sir Christopher stumbled upon the magical field, he was a student at Oxford. He already had an emotional attachment to the place. That's what we've been missing! We can't get the new connections to stabilise because none of us are tied to the other places we've tried."

"My word," Kate utters. "I think you're right. Or, at least, there's a good chance you're on the right path. There's only one way we can find out, and that's by making another attempt."

Kate's answer sends me straight into event planner mode. I organise my thoughts. "How strong is Lavinia's connection to Padua?"

"Her family has lived there for as many generations back as she can trace. And Lavinia once told me it was Padua's famous frescos that inspired her early love of art."

"I don't think we'll find anyone better than that," I agree. "Should we take a risk and tell Lavinia about the existence of magic? How do you think she'd react?"

"Truthfully, I have no idea. Lavinia's always been pragmatic." Kate pauses, tapping her chin. "However, more than once, I have caught her tossing a sprinkle of salt over her shoulder to ward off bad luck."

Mathilde pipes up, joining into the discussion. "Italian literature is full of otherworldly suspicions and old wives' tales, not to mention all the examples of so-called divine intervention. It wouldn't surprise me if the Eternals there were somehow managing to inspire and instruct Italians throughout history. That might make our task even simpler. The strong bond between the Eternals and the living, combined with the right instruments to stabilise the connection... we'd be foolish to let this opportunity slip past us."

I check everyone's faces, scanning to see if anyone has doubts they've left unvoiced. But there are no muddled expressions or frowns. In fact, for the first time in a while, I can sense a palpable excitement in the air.

"That settles it. We're all going to Padua." I reach into my handbag and pull out a notepad and pen. "I'll start a To Do list for each of us. Mathilde, put in your time-off request and ask the Eternals to use their influence to get it approved. Kate, can you call Lavinia and make sure she'll be around?" I scratch down my notes as fast as I can. "Let's see... what else? Travel arrangements and lodging! Harry, I presume you don't mind making the bookings for us?"

Harry smiles, clearly happy to be involved in the activities this time around. "If we're all going, maybe a short-let flat would be a better option than a hotel."

Mathilde clears her throat, causing me to pause my writing. "That covers the rest of us, Nat, but what are you going to do?"

"I've got the hardest task of all, Mathilde. I've got to figure out how to get a wyvern onto an airplane."

Chapter Three

Heathrow Airport seems particularly busy on the afternoon of our departure. I'm not sure whether that is an advantage or potentially catastrophic. That all depends on a certain scaly wyvern who is currently huddling inside my bag. He isn't much larger than a cat, but with dark grey wings, yellow eyes, and fiery breath, he certainly doesn't fit the mould of the typical airline pet. His magical connection ensures anyone outside our little group sees him as a black cat with white spots, but even a cat would be out of place in a departure lounge.

H behaves remarkably well as Harry, Mathilde, and I queue for the check-in counter. He keeps quiet as we show our passports and lift our suitcases onto the belt for tagging. His good nature ends when we are standing awkwardly in the middle of the airport, arguing over the best way to sneak an animal through security.

"I don't understand why you didn't declare him and bring him on like a regular animal!" Harry grumbles. "Couldn't you have said he was your emotional support cat?"

I roll my eyes, familiar with the argument. It isn't the first time she's raised the idea. "I told you, Harry, H is too big to fit in the tiny cat carriers, and can you imagine me walking him on a leash?"

H sends a puff of smoke swirling from the top of my bag. "Iffen you think I'm going to walk around like some fur-brained dog, you've lost your loaf, for sure!"

"No one is going to treat you like a dog, H," I reassure him, reaching a hand into my bag to pat his head. "Can everyone pipe down for a moment and let me think? Actually, wait here. I'm going to circle around to the other side of the entrance to the security checkpoint so H can get a closer look."

I leave Harry and Mathilde standing there, other passengers swerving around them in their rush to catch their flights. At least time isn't a problem. We've arrived well in advance to make sure we have plenty of leeway to deal with any unexpected issues that might arise. When travelling with a wyvern, the unexpected is inevitable.

I dodge a teary couple who cling to each other as they say their goodbyes. Seeing them gives me a brief pang as I think about my fiancé, whom I've left at home. "It's only ten days," I remind myself before the doldrums set in. Independent woman or not, this was the first time we've been apart for more than a weekend since we started dating.

"Nat, you're squeezing me so 'ard I can't breathe in 'ere," H croaks.

"Oops, sorry," I reply. I shift my arm so that the bag is angled to the front. H raises his head high enough that one yellow eye peeks over the edge. I nod towards the line of people standing across the way and wait for H to take a good look. "It's just like the videos we watched, H. All the bags go through the x-ray machine, while the people step through the metal detector. You're going to have to sneak through. Which of our potential plans do you think will work best?"

H takes his time surveying the space. I can see my worries

have been for nothing. While H is antic-prone, he is taking his first trip outside of the UK very seriously. After spending four centuries in Oxford, he isn't going to do anything which might mess up his chances of seeing something new in the world.

Finally, he snorts and speaks. "There's a small crawl space under the x-ray belt. It will be a tight fit, but iffen I keep my wings tucked in, I think I can fit."

I take a last look, but nothing better comes to mind. "It will have to work, because I can't see any other way. Is your collar in place?"

H uses a talon to show me the gold coin hanging from a leather strap around his narrow neck. Once we received detailed information on Oxford's connection to the magical field around Earth, the Eternals had spent weeks experimenting with how it worked. Along the way, they figured out how to make a portable connection which would allow H to travel outside of Oxford's borders without being trapped in his cat form. Kate offered a gold medallion from the Ashmolean's collection, and a few days later, H was finally free to see the world. To say he is ecstatic about it is an understatement. Even now, he has it clutched tightly in his claws, not daring to risk that it might get lost.

I take a deep breath and then wave for Harry and Mathilde to join me. "Here goes nothing!"

Everything starts off well. Harry goes in front of me, Mathilde bringing up the rear. The two of them are ready to jump in with a distraction if anything goes wrong. I glance back, relieved to see Mathilde looking as cool as a cucumber. You'd think she snuck magical creatures through airport security regularly. Harry, however, shifts nervously. Normally calm and collected in the face of most any challenge, apparently wyverns in airports are past her breaking point.

"Take your large electronics out of your bags and put everything into a tray," the security guard shouts, his voice rising above the hum of the crowd. We shuffle forward, winding around the barriers as we make our way to the front. Harry is the first to arrive at the belt. She launches into a flurry of questions, pretending as though she's never been in an airport before. While the security guard and everyone around us are distracted, I kneel and let H crawl out of my bag, while pretending to tie my shoelaces.

"See you on the other side," I whisper, giving his head a quick stroke. He squares his shoulders, tucks his wings in as tight as possible, and slips under the table and out of sight.

We are so close to getting away with it.

It is Harry who gives us away in the end. She doesn't mean to, of course. But her frayed nerves have left her off-kilter enough that she accidentally bumps into someone else and sets off a chain reaction.

Harry goes through the metal detector first. She clears it without any problems, although I am amazed the security team doesn't flag her for an extra check. She is bobbing from side-to-side, antsy to get away from the checkpoint. I give her a stern look before motioning her towards the other end of the x-ray belt. All she has to do is pick up her handbag and head on her way.

But then I cause the metal detector to beep. With all my thoughts focused on getting H through, I forget to take off my watch. It is a simple enough problem to solve, but when Harry hears the metallic beeping noise, she leaps sideways and bumps into the young woman next to her. The poor young woman, hands full with her overflowing tray of personal items, can do little more than stare in shock as her tray tips forward and spills everything onto the floor.

"Oh, my goodness! I'm so sorry!" Harry cries, bending over to help the stranger collect her things.

"That's okay," the young woman replies, tucking her hair

behind her ears so she can search around. Her handbag was open, and everything inside it is now spread across the floor. She kneels in time to see a small gold tube roll across the floor. She lunges, exclaiming in horror, "My new lipstick!"

H, bless him, is in the right place at the right time to save the woman from losing her expensive make-up. I watch as a familiar black claw swipes out from under the table, knocking the lipstick back towards its owner.

"Cheers," the young woman replies, on autopilot. The words are barely out of her mouth before her brain clicks in. "Wait, was that a cat? Is there a cat under the conveyor belt?"

I rip my watch from my arm and pass it to Mathilde, dashing through the metal detector as quick as I can. Harry's face pales and she nearly swoons before I get to her side.

"A cat?" I gasp, my tone conveying how ridiculous the idea was. "How would a cat get underneath there?"

If we were in Oxford, the magic of the town would have prevented anyone from thinking anything strange about finding a cat in the middle of a busy airport. But we aren't in Oxford, and H's personal magical field doesn't extend much beyond his body. It is enough to make people think he is a cat, but that is it.

Here at Heathrow, it is too late. The damage is done. Everyone around us is bent over, doing their best to peer under the small gap beneath the conveyer belt stand. There is no way to sneak H out without a dozen people bearing witness. Fortunately, H and I have come prepared with a back-up plan.

I murmur the words *sausage roll* loud enough for H to hear, and then elbow my way to the conveyor belt to claim my items. As soon as I move into place, I shout that my watch is missing.

"It's not here. Someone must have stolen it!" I send frantic glances at everyone, practically begging them for help. My distraction works, and while the security guards and other passengers turn their attention to helping me with my problem, H shoots out from under the table.

The poor young woman who'd spilled her tray is the only one to see him dash off. H runs as fast as his little legs can take him, pumping his wings as he waits for an empty space to take off into the air.

"The cat..." the woman blurts, a dumbfounded look on her face. "It... it flew... a flying cat..." She sways on her feet and turns pale, overcome with shock.

Harry, finally out of her own stupor, wraps an arm around the woman's shoulders and helps her to a nearby chair. "Perhaps you should take a seat, dear. Do you get low blood sugar? I'm sure I've got some sweeties in my handbag."

After H's getaway and Harry's intervention, Mathilde and I set to work calming the situation. I find my watch, and Mathilde helps me gather the rest of our items. Any lingering questions or doubts about what has happened fade as both fellow passengers and security guards alike are simply happy to see us get out of the way.

Harry, Mathilde, and I make a brisk getaway, no one daring to say a word until we have put the security checkpoint well behind us.

"How will we find H again?" Harry asks, looking very guilty.

"He should be hiding under a table in the food hall," I answer, hoping he made it to safety. "That was our plan, anyway."

"You'd better get out your purse, Harry," Mathilde suggests, bumping Harry's arm. "Accident or not, you nearly got us caught. H will have worked up quite an appetite during his panicked flight to safety."

I snicker, leaning around Harry to catch Mathilde's eye. "And now you know why H and I called the back-up plan Operation Sausage Roll."

Sure enough, H is safely ensconced under a chair in the far corner of the food hall. Finding him is easy enough. All I have to do is keep an eye out for a little trail of smoke and there he is.

"Come on, mate," I urge in an apologetic voice. "Harry has promised to treat you to a sausage roll or pasty — your choice."

"It's the least I can do. In fact, I probably owe half the terminal a coffee after that nonsense. I just kept imagining us being dragged away in handcuffs," Harry admits.

Although I know she is serious, the thought of Harry, with her white hair, emerald sweater, and practical black trousers, being carted off with a snarling cat in her arms is too much for me. I burst out laughing and Mathilde follows right behind me. Before long, all of us are laughing so hard that we have to wipe our eyes.

"All's well that ends well, right?" I offer H my bag and he climbs back inside with nary a whinge.

H settles comfortably, with his snout poking out the top. "I wasn't keen on the idea of stayin' in a bag for 'ours when we first set off, but I'm startin' to see the benefits of 'aving a 'iding spot, iffen you know what I mean."

"We've got an hour to kill before boarding starts. What do you say to a round of coffees while we wait?" Harry gathers her handbag and heads off to order, leaving the rest of us at the table.

"Don't forget some pasties!" H croaks, causing a few heads to turn our way. I shush him before people stare and we have to make a mad dash.

Mathilde raps on the table, pulling H's attention back our way. "So H, how are you feeling about your first airline flight?"

H stares at her, smoke curling from his nostril. "I fly all the time, Tildy. I've got wings, remember?"

I bite my lip to keep from laughing at his deadpan look.

"Skimming above people's heads isn't the same thing as soaring at 30,000 feet, H."

"I won't be feelin' the breeze under my wings, though, Nat," H corrects me. "I'm more excited about what comes after we land, missies. An 'ole other country!" His yellow eyes glitter. "I never dared to dream about seein' somethin' other than Oxford. This is bigger and better than anythin' I could ever imagine."

Seeing the happiness and wonder play across his face, I decide then and there that this won't be H's last trip abroad. He deserves to see the world as much as anyone else. Maybe more so, if I'm being honest.

H's enthusiasm fades as we stand in an endless queue waiting to board our plane. I cross my fingers and toes while the gate agent scans our tickets and checks our passports. But finally, we make it into the relative safety of the airplane. We're seated three in a row, me at the window, Mathilde in the middle, and Harry at the aisle. H is lounging in the bag near my feet.

We thought long and hard about which seats to reserve. Now that we're here, I'm pleased with our choice. Lost in the endless middle of the plane, other passengers and flight attendants stride past us with nary a glance. As far as they know, we're nothing more than three women on a business trip.

It takes some fancy footwork at times, and all our free airplane snacks, but we somehow keep H hidden during the short flight to the Venice airport. As we descend for our final approach, it's worth every sweat drop and frayed nerve, however, to watch his yellow eyes glow when he sees the top of St Mark's Belltower in Venice dotting the skyline in the distance.

"Look at it, Nat," he whispers, using a talon to point at the window. "It's nothin' like England. Seems like somethin' from a fairy tale. I can't believe there's no magic there."

"If anyplace on Earth has magic, I suspect it is Venice," Mathilde says, leaning close so she can see as well. "Hopefully, we'll have time to fit in a quick visit. It would be a shame to come so close without taking advantage of the opportunity to see Venice's grand canal and famous bridges."

"It's only half an hour by train, if I'm remembering what I read correctly. Surely we can spare a day over the weekend," I suggest, already savouring the thought. I pull out my phone and type the event into my calendar. "It's a plan."

Harry nods her agreement, but I notice Mathilde is awfully quiet.

I wonder whether Mathilde is missing home. Or someone she left at home. Her relationship with DI Trevor Robinson is even newer than my relationship. "Why aren't you more excited?"

"Oh, I am excited," Mathilde replies, but her smile is wary. "It's nothing... really."

Now Harry is as concerned as I am. "It's clearly not nothing, Mathilde. What's on your mind?"

Seeing she's caught our attention, Mathilde takes a deep breath and admits, "We've got a tremendous challenge in front of us... telling someone else about magic, putting the pieces in place to forge a connection, meeting new Eternals. We haven't even stopped to think what we'll do if our attempt to connect to the magic fails."

The seatbelt sign turns off with a ding, preventing me from replying. As we gather our carry-on items and I help H get comfortable in his carrier bag, my mind is spinning with a realisation.

Mathilde is right to be concerned. Our introduction to magic was far from smooth. We shouldn't arrive in Padua naively, thinking all will go perfectly. There are bound to be some bumps along the way.

I catch Mathilde's eye as we exit the plane. "As long as we don't stumble across any dead bodies, I am sure we can handle whatever life and magic throw our way."

As I consider the words that just came out of my mouth, I realise how ridiculous I sound. Most people go their whole life without encountering a crime. What happened to us in the past year in Oxford was a rarity. Still, the idea of stumbling across another dead body gives me a sense of foreboding.

I shake my head and focus on anything else.

As we stand in a crowded mass of people waiting for our passports to be checked, H squirms uncomfortably in my bag. I hoarsely whisper a word of warning when it is my turn to face the customs agent, and nearly give a cheer when I'm finally cleared to continue to baggage claim.

The baggage claim is spacious and well-lit, making a pleasant change from the customs area. Passengers trickle in as they pass through customs, quickly staking their claim to a place beside the luggage belt. Despite being in a terribly uninspiring setting, I can't help feeling a swirl of excitement in my stomach. From the Italian language on all the signage, to the posters promoting day trips to Venice, everywhere I look there is some small reminder that I'm not in England anymore.

H seems equally wondrous, his yellow eyes open wide as his head twists from side to side. What must it feel like to leave the UK for the first time in such a long existence? I haven't been to Italy before, either, but I know it's not the same. No matter what happens, this will be a trip we'll never forget.

Gradually, my enthusiasm dies down as we're stuck cooling our heels beside the baggage carousel. Mathilde, Harry, and I regroup while we wait for our suitcases to appear.

"Why don't we take turns popping to the loo before we go outside to meet Kate," Harry suggests, ever the practical one. I pass H's bag into Mathilde's outstretched arms and make a beeline for the restroom sign.

When I return a few minutes later, the first thing I notice is Mathilde's absence. Harry is right where I left her, her full attention concentrated on the baggage claim belt.

"Um, Harry," I stutter worriedly. "Where did Mathilde and H go? I hope he didn't cause any trouble." Before she can reply, a familiar snout passes in front of me on the moving carousel. H is stretched out, his face the very picture of glee as he glides past us, waving a wing in my direction. I send a shocked glance around and am amazed to see that no one seems concerned.

"They think he's an airport stray," Harry explains. "Mathilde and I didn't see the harm in letting him enjoy himself for a few minutes. We assumed you'd agree."

"How can I say no when he looks that happy?" I reply, laughing. H manages a few more trips around before the buzzer sounds and the first suitcase appears. He leaps to safety in time to avoid being smashed by the baggage sliding onto the belt.

Mathilde's and my luggage are among the first to arrive. Recognising H's desperate need to get out of the airport, Harry waves us on. "Kate texted that she and her friend are waiting outside Arrivals. Why don't you three go find them while I wait for my suitcase? You can leave your luggage on the cart, if you'd like."

Only the reminder that we still have to clear the live animal checkpoint convinces H to get back inside my bag one last time. As soon as we pass the last set of automatic doors, he burns a hole in the side and flies free to land by my feet, barely giving the magic time to repair my bag.

My load now much lighter, I stop for a moment to take in my surroundings. Fresh brewed espresso lightly perfumes the air, pairing perfectly with the giant adverts hanging from the ceiling, showing supermodels in ballgowns sipping from demitasse cups.

Although we're at the airport, there is still a hint of Italy in the white stone floor and red brick walls. The aesthetic is somehow both utilitarian and elegant.

"Nat! Mathilde! Yoohoo!" Kate's sharp English vowels cut through the singsong Italian burble in the terminal.

There are taxi drivers holding signs with names written in clumsy handwriting. I spy a couple of women wearing brightly coloured blazers calling for cruise ship passengers. More than a few Italian families are enthusiastically welcoming back loved ones. But nowhere in the mix is Kate.

Finally, a waving arm catches my eye. Kate, with her dark hair cut into a chic bob, wearing an artsy, all-black ensemble with only a designer scarf to provide a dash of flair, has perfectly blended in with the other Italian families. Between Mathilde's snarky t-shirt and denim skirt, and my polka-dot jumpsuit, there isn't a chance of us doing the same.

Kate pulls us into a quick hug and kisses both our cheeks, giving us an induction into the Italian way of saying hello.

"Hullo, H!" she croons, scratching his chin. "I see you made it here safely."

"He did, but I'm not sure about my sanity," I mumble, making both Kate and Mathilde laugh.

When Kate stands up straight, I notice the woman standing beside her. She's similar in height to Kate, with the light brown hair and sun-kissed skin often seen in Northern Italians. She, too, is wearing a monochromatic look, accessorising with a statement necklace instead of a scarf. With their similar style and stance, she and Kate could be bookends. I don't have to think hard to guess who she is.

"You must be Lavinia," I say, offering my hand. "I'm Natalie Payne, but please call me Nat."

"Piacere," she replies before leaning in to kiss my cheeks as well. "Welcome to Italy, Nat. I've heard so much about you from

Kate. I feel as though I know you already." Her accent is melodic as she introduces herself to Mathilde and takes in the sight of H brushing his head against my leg. "When you said they were bringing a cat, I didn't believe you, Kate."

"H is quite the unusual character, Lavinia," Kate replies, giving me a wink. That's an understatement, if I've ever heard one.

Lavinia gives H another glance, trying to figure out if there is some deeper meaning to Kate's words. But all she can see is a black cat with two white spots and bright yellow eyes staring up at her. Even H's hello comes across as a loud miaow. His magic might be hidden from sight, but his charm is still apparent. Lavinia gives in and pets him on the head.

"Aren't we expecting one more?" Lavinia asks, looking around for the missing member of our party.

"Yes, Harry," I reply. "She was waiting on her suitcase, but should be right behind us." I shift around to stand beside Lavinia and Kate, giving me a clear view of the passengers exiting the security area. Within seconds, I spot Harry's white blonde head bobbing along with the crowd as she pushes the luggage cart. "There she is!"

Harry's introduction proceeds more quickly. We fall into line with the crowd of passengers moving towards the exit sign. Outside, Lavinia pauses on the pavement to point us in the right direction.

"My car is parked in the short stay lot you can see in the distance." She sets off to the zebra crossing, navigating her way between a lane of taxis waiting to collect people.

"Look left," Kate reminds us, barely getting the words out before a taxi nearly mows us down. "Every time I venture outside of the UK, it takes my brain a day or two to remember which way to check."

Looking the wrong way isn't my issue. I'm looking everywhere — at the people walking near us, at the makes and models of the cars parked up ahead, and mostly at H, who is flying circles around us in his excitement. Somehow, we make it across the taxi lane and the bus lane beyond it, finally arriving at the edge of an asphalt car park.

Harry spots a line of luggage carts and calls us over to collect our bags. Harry takes her bag from the top, then Mathilde, and finally I get mine from the bottom. H swoops in for a closer look, his wings ruffling Harry's hair as he shaves past her. She throws up an arm to wave him off, and staggers sideways.

My attention stays fixed on H, as I chastise him for his bad behaviour. But he ignores me, circling around to fly behind Harry. Before I can shout at him, I realise his actions have a purpose. Still off balance, Harry has nearly stumbled into the busy street, and only H's timely intervention has saved her from what could have been a nasty accident with a fast-moving taxicab.

I rush to her side, wanting to reassure her as much as myself. "Goodness, Harry! Are you okay?"

"I'm fine," she replies in a bewildered tone, looking around at the pavement. "I must have caught my heel on something. I just couldn't seem to right myself."

I follow her gaze, wondering what could have tripped her up, but there is nothing there. The pavement is smooth, with nary a crack to cause trouble.

Harry's frown deepens as she cannot find a reasonable explanation for what happened.

Not wanting her to worry, I wrap an arm around her shoulder and gently nudge her towards her suitcase. "Maybe your blood sugar is low. I know just the thing to fix that."

"What's that?" she asks.

"A big scoop of gelato. Come on. Let's ask Kate's friend if she knows a place we can stop on the way to Padua."

Chapter Four

The next morning arrives with the sun shining on a glorious autumn day. Having woken earlier than the rest, I take a moment of quiet to gaze out my bedroom window at the streets surrounding the flat we rented. Already, my heart thrums with excitement over the possibilities of what we may find. We're scheduled to tour the city, and we intend to take full advantage of the opportunity to learn more about the history of Padua and its inhabitants before we broach the topic of magic with Lavinia.

We spent the evening before preparing ourselves, each in our own way. I had pulled out my notebook and coloured pens, putting together lists of how we should react to potential problems. I feel better going into our conversation with Lavinia knowing I've got fallback plans should she react poorly, or should we fail to stabilise the connection.

Kate also made lists, although her's were of a very different nature. Telling her friend Lavinia that magic is real won't be easy. I don't blame her for wanting to get her thoughts in order.

Mathilde discovered a tome-sized guide to the history of Padua sitting on the bookshelf in our short-let flat, and disappeared into her room, with H to keep her company.

Only Harry enjoyed a relaxing evening. With the rest of us occupied, she curled up on the sofa with a new mystery novel and a glass of red wine. I tried not to envy her, but it was a losing battle.

Soon enough, I hear movement coming from the other bedrooms, and heels clicking in the hallway. We take turns in the bathroom, not yet accustomed to sharing space with one another. I think little of it when H scoffs a creme-filled croissant without bothering to chew it. But when he drops my shoes at my feet and insists I get a move on it, I can't help but wonder what has him so excited.

He hustles the four of us women out the door of our flat, only slowing enough to allow Kate to take the lead once we get outside onto the pavement. In the morning sunlight, the pastel-painted buildings take on a warm glow. I spy buttery yellow and pale pink tones, the calming colours providing an intriguing juxtaposition with the busy street. Men in tight-fitting suits chatter into their phones while women in impossibly high heels expertly navigate the cobblestones.

I've come prepared to spend the day walking the streets as we get to know the town. My clothing is comfortable, my trainers are well-worn, and my handbag is packed with all the essentials. My phone is in hand, ready to take photos of the sights. If I happen to photograph a few shop windows along the way, it will be understandable. Everywhere I look there is a detail, some tiny and some large, which begs to be captured by my lens.

"Our first stop this morning is the Basilica di Sant'Antonio... or as the Padovani call it, il Santo." Kate double-checks the directions on her phone. "Lavinia is going to meet us there, so let's be on our way."

Harry and Kate lead our group, their heads close together as they coordinate their plans. While it feels like a tourist visit, there is plenty of work to be done. From what I can hear, the women are already comparing and contrasting the city centre with that of Oxford.

"Neither Oxford nor Padua have what people think of as the traditional university campus," Kate explains, glancing over her shoulder to include Mathilde, H, and me as well. "The universities and the towns are inextricably linked. One obvious difference, however, is in their admissions process. Whereas Oxford is highly selective and attracts students from around the world, youth in Italy typically attend the university closest to their home. Not always," she amends, "but most of the time. Personally, I think it intertwines the town, the people, and the university even tighter. Students truly think of this as their home."

On that lovely sentiment, Kate forges ahead, commenting on the time and our need to hurry if we don't want to be late.

As the others pull ahead, I grab a hold of H's back leg, slowing him down. "What has got into you this morning? You are far too excited about seeing some old buildings."

H tucks his head in tight, looking sheepish. "Tildy said somethin' last night about a cat statue sittin' in front of the Basilica. A female cat! What if it's another Eternal?"

As excited as he is, I can't help but feel somewhat dubious. "A cat statue in front of a catholic church... are you sure you heard her correctly?"

H nods his head feverishly. "She kept saying gatta — that's Italian for cat, you know."

"Wait a minute," I stutter to a halt. "You can speak Italian?"

"'Course I can, missie. I'm an Eternal. I wouldn't be much good iffen I couldn't communicate with people." H rolls his eyes at my naivety.

For his sake, I hope he's right. We speed up, catching up with the rest of the group. Within a few minutes, Kate guides us towards a large piazza. H's head swivels from side-to-side, searching everywhere for his new best friend.

"Can we take a closer look at the statue?" Mathilde asks, pointing at a bronze statue which sits atop a towering pedestal. The statue captures a man and horse poised to be admired. The man's back is straight and the horse's head is angled to the side, every detail cast to perfection. "It's by Donatello, himself, and dates back to the 1450s. Isn't it stunning?"

"Yeah, yeah, Tildy..." H motions for her to wrap up her impromptu presentation. "But where's the gatta statue?"

Mathilde cocks her head to the side. "Right here. I just showed it to you. The hero riding the horse was known as the Gattamelata. It was his nickname," she adds when H cannot be convinced. H's scowl deepens, his disappointment clear. Even the thought of making friends with a warhorse isn't enough to offset the loss of a potential Eternal cat.

My heart gives a lurch for my scaly, little friend. "Come on, mate. Let's go into the church. I hear they've got Saint Anthony's incorruptible tongue stored in a box. Maybe that will be interesting?" H grumbles, but comes along, staying close to our group so that he can pass unnoticed.

We find Lavinia waiting inside. She raises an eyebrow when she spots H, but Kate gestures for her to keep quiet. Lavinia gives a small shake of her head, but does as Kate asks, launching into a whispered tour of the frescoed chapels for which the Basilica is famed.

We wander through the church, keeping out of the way of robed priests who are going about their business. Padua is a pilgrimage sight, attracting both casual visitors like us and the devout. Even on a random autumn weekday, the church grounds are busy.

"This is where the relics are on display," Lavinia explains, motioning to a room up ahead. We pause in front of a large display board which tells the story of Saint Anthony and how his relics came to be housed in Padua. While everyone's attention is on the board, I notice H is looking in the opposite direction, smoke leaking from his nostrils.

"Everything okay?" I ask in a low whisper.

H gives the room a scan before replying, "'Ave you noticed anyone starin' at us? I can feel eyes trackin' my every step."

Only the sharp glint in his eye prevents me from brushing off his remark. I bend down beside him, checking out the view from his level. There are a few people milling around, but no one seems to look our way. "H, you're a cat walking in a cathedral. Although we're doing our best to keep you hidden in the group, I'm sure at least a couple of people must have noticed you."

H gives me a long look, searching my face, before deciding I must be right. However, as our group moves away from the information boards, I notice him tucking in tighter between us.

We climb a short rise of stairs to reach the display level. There, glass windows protect the jewelled boxes and vases from being handled. No one speaks, the heavy atmosphere stifling any desire to say a word. We file past the displays, Kate and Lavinia in the front, Mathilde gliding behind. H keeps close to my side, not wanting to attract the attention of the priest standing watch over the space. Harry, hanging back, takes her time as she looks carefully at each item, reading the accompanying explanation cards.

We leave Harry in peace, our little group gathering at the base of the small set of stairs to wait for her. I don't mind the delay. I spend the time wondering what sort of Eternals could be walking amongst us. Would they be priests and nuns? Or am I more likely to find supplicants and devout worshippers? With any luck, we might soon find out.

Harry's whispered apology recalls my attention to the present. "Sorry, ladies. I didn't realise I was holding everyone up." She bustles along the narrow walkway in front of the cases to the top of the four steps leading back to the ground. In her rush, her foot slips on the smooth marble step, and she shrieks in surprise as she grabs at the air. Her arms windmill and her navy coat billows out like wings, but it is of no use. Harry pitches forward, plunging face first towards the unyielding stone floor of the chapel.

I move without conscious thought, my body leaping into action before my brain can even process what is happening. Harry tumbles into my arms, sending me stumbling backwards as her weight throws me off balance. The two of us land in a heap on the chapel floor.

"Signore!" the priest cries, rushing over to us to see if we're injured as we untangle ourselves. Had the stairs been any higher, one of us would have surely been hurt. But thanks to my quick action, and the bulk of my handbag, we seem to be unscathed. Mathilde and Kate help us to our feet as Lavinia speaks to the priest in a rush of Italian.

"Nat, are you okay?" Harry asks, her voice high-pitched with worry as she checks herself in disbelief.

"I'm fine," I reassure her. "My coat and handbag got the worst of it. I knew packing my notebook and scarf was a good idea. They cushioned my fall. Are you all right?"

Harry is shaking, her lips pressed tightly together. "I'm not hurt, but Nat... someone pushed me!"

"Pushed you?" I stare at her, the words not computing. "There was no one close to you, Harry."

Harry pales even further, standing in stark contrast to her bright pink scarf as her eyes dart around the room. I don't know what she expects to see. There is no one here but our group and the old priest. She freezes in place, staring at the marble steps, their edges worn smooth by centuries of visitors plodding over them. Sliding off the edge of one would be perfectly understandable.

Her eyes narrow, her gaze lost in the distance. "I'm sure I felt someone shove my shoulder, Nat. I can't explain it, but I really don't think it was as simple as me losing my balance."

Mathilde and I exchange worried looks while Harry continues to stare at the steps. We have no reason not to believe Harry is telling the truth, but equally, no alternative explanation that would make sense. While we know Eternals exist, without a connection between their plane of existence and ours, it seems impossible that one could be involved.

Harry reaches the same conclusion as the rest of us, her shoulders falling as she sighs. "Maybe you're right. Maybe I slipped."

As I gather myself, a feeling of dread creeps in again. H catches my eye and reads my expression. He nods slightly, indicating he is feeling the same way.

Lavinia suggests we retreat to a nearby cafe for a hot drink. As we leave the chapel behind, my mind is filled with worries. Something is clearly going on with Harry.

Lavinia proves to be a wonderful tour guide as she shows off her city. After a light lunch at an outdoor cafe in one of Padua's principal squares, she announces it is time to visit the university.

"Palazzo del Bo is the official seat of the university," she explains as we stand in front of a stone-lined arched entrance to a large building. "Within its halls, Galileo lectured students on the wonders of the sky, the first female university graduate in the world received her diploma, and the field of anatomy laid its roots."

Suitably impressed, we follow her inside. Unlike the Oxford colleges, there is no security team poised at the entrance, waiting to check IDs or sell admission. With over sixty-thousand students, the university is three times larger than Oxford. Its doors are open to any and everyone who wishes to pursue knowledge. In the case of Palazzo del Bo, the term applies even in the most literal sense.

Whereas Oxford's walls are home to gargoyles and paintings, Palazzo del Bo is festooned with family crests. Lavinia explains that the coats of arms represent the families of the faculty and students who attended until the 17th century. It is a good reminder for our Oxford group that knowledge was once limited to the wealthy. As the world changed, so too did the educational system. It is only right that the magic should follow suit.

I glance over to see Mathilde staring at the wall, her lips moving as she reads a Latin inscription. Her delight is apparent and is no surprise. Of all of us, she is the most entrenched in the past, spending so much of her days reading the words of people long dead. For her, this building is like a brand new book, its history written on the walls for anyone with the language skills to read it.

We pause in a square courtyard, letting the sun warm our shoulders after the chill of the stone corridors. Slender white columns line the edge of both the ground and first floor, the architecture reminding me of the cloisters we saw earlier in the day.

Lavinia points to the open hallway above us. "We'll head upstairs now so you can visit the most famous rooms. We'll start with the Sala dei Quaranta." She crosses the courtyard to ascend a monumental staircase. "The statue is of Elena Lucrezia Cornaro Piscopia, the first woman in history to receive a university degree. She was a child prodigy who grew to be a woman so brilliant, the most learned men of the 17th century were forced to acknowledge her capabilities, bestowing upon her a doctorate in philosophy."

Always fascinated by transformative women, I pause in front of the statue to pay my respects. Determined to take a closer look, H leaps into the lap of the diminutive woman who is seated atop a pedestal. No sooner does he land, than the woman herself shakes her head and glances down at him.

"Buongiorno," she announces in a light Italian voice, and slides her stone hand over his head in a gentle caress.

H's eyes grow wider than I ever seen and his head rears back until he releases a huge sneeze. Flames jet from his nostrils, bathing the monument's intricately carved gown in a blanket of fire. I stand aghast, wondering how much damage H's nervous sneeze will cause, but to my shock, it does the opposite. When the flames die out, for a moment, the stone turns to fabric, and the woman laughs in delight.

"How? What?" I stutter, unable to believe what I'm seeing. H, however, is faster on the uptake.

"It's my collar," he explains, gripping the metal coin in his hand. "Since I'm sittin' in 'er lap, she must be able to connect to us."

"Sí, the little creature is right," the woman agrees, her English heavily accented. "How is this possible? How can you see and speak to one another?"

I open my mouth to explain, but before I can speak, the connection falters, and her countenance returns to stone. H tries jumping down and back into her lap, letting his flames lick over the marble, but it is to no avail. By ourselves, we can't stabilise the connection enough to maintain more than a few seconds at a time.

H notes my downcast expression and flies up to hover near my head. "Don't feel so bad, missie. At least we know there are Eternals 'ere in Padua."

"That's true, H," I agree, forcing a smile back onto my face. "You're right to focus on the positive side. Hopefully Lavinia will be the missing piece we need. Now come on, we'd better hurry and catch up with everyone else."

❖

An hour later, I whisper a confession to Mathilde as we finish our tour. "I wish I'd stayed here in the courtyard. Just as I feared, those last two rooms gave me the shivers."

"Really?" She stops in the courtyard and turns around to face me. "I thought the Anatomical Theatre and Medicine Hall were pretty cool. I wouldn't have thought you to be squeamish."

I give Mathilde a hard look. "I wasn't squeamish before I moved to Oxford. However, finding a dead body sprawled across a kitchen table on my first day at work had an impact, you know. After seeing more than my share of dead people, the thought of examining their insides made my stomach churn."

Harry passes by in time to hear my last remark, and pats me on the back. "I don't envy you those experiences, Nat. Let's hope wherever we visit next has a more cheerful atmosphere. After my fall earlier, I could use a pick me up as well." She raises her voice and calls Lavinia's name. "What's next on the agenda?"

"I thought we'd wrap up your first full day in Padova with a local tradition," Lavinia replies, using the Italian name for the city. "After a long day at work, or hours spent studying for exams, we Padovani like nothing better than to meet our friends for an aperitivo."

Her suggestion catches my interest. "Aperitivo? That sounds like the perfect way to take my mind off of death. Where are we going?"

"Not far," Lavinia replies, gesturing for us to follow her. "In fact, I suspect our next stop will particularly interest your cat."

"My cat?" I give H a sideways glance. He is as mystified as I am. "Now I'm really intrigued. Lead the way, Lavinia."

We don't have far to go. After a very short walk, she guides us to a breath-taking, neo-Gothic building. It is hardly what I expected when she proposed we go for happy hour, but then, I shouldn't be surprised that the Italians would celebrate the end of the day in such a style.

The two-story building sits on the edge of a square, with small tables dotted out front. The casual dining area in no way detracts from the grandeur of the building itself. Two covered arcades mark the entrances on either end of the building. Doric columns made of marble climb to an intricately carved relief, lending the building an almost Greek feel. But it isn't the building which captures H's attention. His gaze is riveted on the beasts that guard the front. Four carved lions stretch along the stairs leading to the entrance, sitting like sphinxes guarding a treasure.

H gives me a pleading look, silently asking for permission to make friends with his fellow felines.

"They may not be Eternals," I remind him, but he brushes off my concern, his wings flapping hard as he speeds to the nearest lion. Part of me wants to stay outside and see what happens next, but the siren call of a comfortable chair and relaxing drink win out. I leave H to his exploration and speed to catch up with the other women.

Lavinia points to an empty circular table for four near the window, grabbing an extra chair along the way. We scoot the chairs around and make space, all of us glad to get off our feet.

"If it is okay with everyone, I will order the first round of drinks. I'd like you to try our specialty." Lavinia checks that no one disagrees and then flags down a passing waiter. She trills off our order in Italian, talking so quickly that I don't have a hope of following along.

The waiter returns in short order with five glasses of a bubbly red liquid garnished with olives, and some small bowls of chips and nuts for us to snack upon.

Lavinia explains, "It's one part prosecco, one part sparkling water, and one part Aperol. We call it lo spritz."

While we occupy ourselves with our drinks and snacks, I ask

Lavinia to tell us more about herself. "Kate told us you work in the museum. How did you end up coming back to Padua after studying in England?"

Lavinia settles comfortably in her chair. Today, her light brown hair tumbles artfully over her white buttoned shirt. Her flipped-up collar and tight black trousers are both simple and yet chic. I've always gone my own way when it comes to clothing choices, but I envy her effortless style. You could drop her on any street in the world, and passersby could still identify her as Italian.

"It wasn't in my original plan to return," Lavinia admits, answering my question. "I always wanted to work in the art world, and I left for London imagining I'd end up at Sothebys or the Tate Modern. I studied hard and eventually landed a job at a major player in the international art scene, but something felt off. My mother will tell you I was homesick, but truthfully, as I got a little older, I missed our way of living. I came back to Padova, got married, and started a family. Over time, I realised I could be a better ambassador for my city if I stayed here than I was while I was away."

"Even though none of us grew up in Oxford, I think I speak for all of us when I say we can understand what you mean," I reassure her as Kate, Mathilde, and Harry nod. "What was it like growing up here?"

"It wasn't until I went to liceo, or secondary school as you call it, that I realised just how special Padova is. Usually, the names you study in science class and the art you see in your history books are little more than figures on the page. But here they were all around us. Just think, Galileo stood on our land and stared up at the wonders of the universe. As a moody teen, I would go to the base of the Specola tower and look up at the night sky, and I'd imagine making discoveries of my own. That is the essence of

Padova — it makes the impossible and the fantastical seem within reach."

"After seeing some of the sights today, I would agree that they are within reach." Kate raises her glass and offers a toast. "To Lavinia, for being a fantastic host, and to Padua, for instilling a sense of wonder."

"Cin cin!" Lavinia clinks her glass against each of ours to teach us the Italian toast.

After a few sips, Mathilde takes over the conversation. "Tell us about your family, Lavinia. You have two daughters, is that right?"

"Yes, they are my pride and joy!" Lavinia beams at us, pulling out her phone to show us photos. She tells us about her children and her husband, giving us a peek into her daily life. We order another round of drinks, deciding to try a Bellini this time.

Before long, the conversation segues from Lavinia's children to our own childhood. Even though, except for Kate, we've only known Lavinia for a day, we find an easy camaraderie with one another.

We're midway through a story when Harry's phone rings. "It's Rob, my husband," she explains to Lavinia, before excusing herself from the table. She returns soon enough, all smiles. "Poor man couldn't find the new packet of biscuits in the cupboard. Truthfully, I suspect he is feeling a bit lonely with me away, and this provided him with an excuse to call me."

"My husband is the same way," Lavinia agrees with a knowing smile. "Shall we think about making our way to a restaurant for dinner? What do you fancy?" Lavinia leaves us to debate the options while stepping away to settle our bill at the bar.

"Oh dear," Harry mutters, frantically checking her coat pockets. "This just isn't my day. I seem to have misplaced my scarf. I'm so disappointed, as it was one of my favourites."

"You had it with you at Palazzo del Bo," Mathilde reminds her. "I remember admiring it on the walk over there."

"Yes, you're right," Harry says, looking somewhat relieved. "I took it off when we were standing in the sunshine in the courtyard. It must have fallen out of my pocket. Do you think there's any chance someone turned it in to the information desk?"

"It can't hurt to check." Kate sits back down at the table. "Why don't you dash over and ask? We can wait here."

Harry slips her handbag strap over her shoulder and buttons her coat. "I shouldn't be more than a few minutes. If you want to pick a restaurant, I'm happy to eat whatever you fancy."

"Check on H on your way out, okay?" I call behind her. Harry gives me a wave over her shoulder, confirming she heard my request.

"Now then, where were we?" I ask. "Oh right, dinner. Would it be terrible if I said I wanted pizza again?"

Chapter Five

Harry's absence stretches much longer than any of us expected. When my stomach rumbles, I decide an intervention is needed.

"Surely Harry didn't get lost... should one of us go check on her?" I cast a look at Mathilde, noting her worried frown. "I don't mind going. Do you want to come with me?"

I don't need to ask her twice. Mathilde leaps to her feet and grabs her coat from the back of her chair.

"We'll stay here, just in case she comes in through another door," Lavinia offers, pointing to the other end of the room. "There are several entrances to the caffé, so it's possible she got turned around."

"That makes me feel better. If we run into any trouble, I'll text you, Kate." With that plan in place, Mathilde and I head off.

Outside, H is still busy entertaining himself with the lion statues. He spots Mathilde and me leaving and leaps onto the back of the nearest statue. "Oi, missies... is it time to go?"

Before we can answer, the statue's tail whips through the air and sends H flying towards us. H tumbles, mid-air, but somehow lands gracefully on the back of another lion. It quickly becomes apparent that this is a game they've invented, and not an unwanted attempt at friendship.

Mathilde gasps in shock. "H! Did you connect with the magic?"

H shakes his snout and waves for me to explain. "Not for more than a few seconds at a time. H jumped into the lap of Elena Cornaro's statue at the Palazzo and she was able to say hello. That's what gave H the idea to try with the lions here." We watch them for another second, our smiles growing wider. I slide my arm through Mathilde's and give her a quick squeeze. "The magical field must run very close to the surface here in Padua. This gives me hope that we'll be successful this time."

"I sure hope so," she agrees. Leaving H behind to continue his game, we make the return trip to Palazzo del Bo in less than half the time it took us before. The woman at the information desk is packing her things, but turns to give us her attention when we come rushing through the entrance.

"Sorry to interrupt you, but did you happen to see an older woman come by?" I hold my hand just above my shoulder. "This tall, short white hair, and looking for a scarf? She's one of the visitors from Oxford."

The woman's puzzled expression shifts as recognition flares in her eyes. "Yes, she came by fifteen minutes ago, asking if anyone had turned her scarf in to our lost and found. I was sorry to tell her it hadn't turned up. I believe she was planning to retrace her steps. The rooms should be unlocked for another half hour, if you want to see if you can find her."

"Thanks, we'll do that," I reply. "Should we start from the last place we visited and work back to the start? Knowing how logical Harry is, I bet she'll start from the beginning."

"She is super organised," Mathilde agrees as we climb the stairs. "It's so unlike her to misplace anything. She won't stop looking until she finds it."

The last place we visited inside the palazzo was the medicine hall. I steel myself as we go inside. Lavinia's tales of post mortem investigations are still fresh in my mind. But I needn't have worried. The room is bursting with people, at least twenty, crowded around a tour guide who is explaining the history of the space. Seeing so many tourists taking photos of themselves with the plastic skeletons on display is amusing enough to wipe away my fears.

Mathilde and I split up, edging around the group to make sure Harry isn't tucked away in their midst. We duck and dodge, checking as much for Harry's distinct hair as for any hint of her scarf.

When I reach the far side of the room, I track down Mathilde with my gaze and give her a shake of my head. She motions to the door and I meet her there.

"Anatomical theatre?" she proposes, walking purposefully to the nearest door. I quicken my steps to keep up, barely holding back a groan. The anatomical theatre has six concentric circles of balconies overlooking the autopsy table in the very centre, which gives the room its name. Earlier, we had wandered around each one, Lavinia telling us the history of the theatre as we marvelled at the pristine condition of the four-hundred-year-old space.

Checking each one of those balconies and the walkways behind them will take time. I understand why Harry got delayed.

"Let's look over the edge of the balcony first," Mathilde suggests. "Maybe we'll see her walking around."

Mathilde strides confidently to the balcony on the top level and peers down to the raised wooden plateau that surrounds the autopsy table set deep below us. When she shrieks in horror, I run.

There below us, sprawled over the centuries-old dissection table, lies a woman's body. Despite her nondescript navy coat and the fact that she is face down, there is no doubt in mind who she is. I'd know that white hair anywhere.

"Harry!" I cry, my voice tinged with hysteria. It echoes off the hard wooden surfaces, filling the room like an eerie chant. There's no softness here to absorb the sound. The harsh tones fracture my nerves. Her name bursts forth from my lips again, even higher pitched and louder than before. "Harry! Harry!"

Frantic, I spin around, desperately trying to remember where I can find the stairs which will take me to the ground level of the theatre. I burst into the outer hall and run straight into someone else.

"Nat?" the voice asks, breathy in panic. "What's wrong?"

I can hardly breathe as I realise what I'm seeing. Harry, in the flesh, looking hearty and hale, albeit full of concern.

She blinks at me, somewhat out of breath, as though she'd come running when she heard my scream. "Why were you shouting my name? What's happened?"

Mathilde, hot on my heels, ploughs through the door and sweeps Harry into an unexpected embrace. "Oh god, Harry! I thought it was you!"

"Thought what was me? What has got into you two?" Harry tries to disentangle herself from Mathilde's arms. "I'm fine except for you squeezing me half to death. You two are scaring me. Has something happened to Kate? Or H?"

"Kate or H?" My eyebrows shoot up, her words making me near delirious. "There's a woman in the theatre. We thought she was you?"

"What?" Harry grabs my arm and nearly drags me inside. She hurries to the balcony to peer down, her gasp audible as she sees what we saw only moments earlier. "My word! Is she... wait, her arm is moving. She isn't dead! We've got to help her!"

Whereas Mathilde and I had lost ourselves to shock and an outpouring of our emotions, Harry's cooler head prevails. She doesn't hesitate, winding down the levels of the theatre until she reaches the ground floor.

❖

The woman has hardly moved, and I fear Harry was mistaken. But then I hear a faint groan coming from the direction of the centre of the room. Harry, several steps ahead of me, is the first to arrive. She wraps an arm around the woman and helps her slide to the floor.

Now that they are side-by-side, I can see an obvious difference. The woman's hair is longer than Harry's and her coat is the wrong colour. However, puddled beside her, is a familiar pink scarf. Harry notices it as well.

"My scarf! How did it end up here?" She shoves it towards Mathilde and returns her attention to the poor woman lying beside her. Her breathing is ragged as she wraps her arms tight around herself.

"Oof, mijn hoofd en mijn ribben!" the stranger moans in Dutch, one hand raising up to her forehead.

"Nat, go see if you can find someone who works here," Harry orders in a no-nonsense tone. She is firmly in control, her voice calm as she reassures the injured woman that help is on the way.

My hands are still shaking as I sprint for the door. I spot another doorway a little further along the hallway and make a beeline for it. The handle twists smoothly in my hand, thankfully unlocked, and the door opens to reveal a small office. There are three people inside, all students I guess.

Seated around a table covered in open laptops and stacks of papers, they are clearly hard at work and not at all happy to be interrupted. However, their initial annoyance turns to concern when they see the look on my face.

"Please, we need help. Someone has been hurt!" I half-shout, my adrenaline still rushing through my veins.

The young female student leaps into action, shoving back her chair so she can reach the phone on the desk behind her. She presses a few keys and then listens until someone answers at the other end. "C'é stato un incidente e ci serve aiuto... sí, un attimo," she puts her hand over the phone and asks, "Dove? Where?"

"We're in the anatomical theatre," I reply. I leave her to finish the call, exiting the room to lead the two men from the office back to the scene. "Are either of you doctors, by any chance?"

"No," the blond man replies in impeccable English. "We're medical historians, but we'll do what we can until security arrives."

I stand aside, letting them help Harry. Mathilde gestures for me to join her, and the two of us shift awkwardly in place, both of us wanting to help but neither of us knowing what to do. The woman has a goose-egg growing in the middle of her forehead, and her breathing is ragged.

One student sets off to get a bag of ice from a nearby break room after the female student arrives with a blanket. Harry helps the Dutch woman lie on her side when she complains that the room is spinning.

"Rest here for a minute. Is there anyone we can call for you?" Harry asks gently.

"Yes, my husband," she answers, her voice weak. "We were in a tour group. He must be worried by now."

Knowing the building better than any of us, the trio of students offer to find the group and retrieve the woman's husband.

Haltingly, the woman describes her husband's appearance and then adds, "His name is Martijn Bakker."

Harry rubs the woman's shoulder, assuring her the students will be back before she knows it. While Harry is doing everything she can to convey positive sentiments, I can't help being worried.

"There's no way this was an accident," I whisper to Mathilde.

Although I was keeping my voice low, Harry overhears my thoughts. "Mrs Bakker, I don't want to upset you, but I need to ask. Did someone attack you?"

Mrs Bakker's eyes fill with tears and she moans again, clearly distraught.

Harry motions her to keep still. "No, don't move. You don't have to tell us anything yet if you aren't up to it."

"No, no," Mrs Bakker answers, wiping her tears away with a tissue Harry gives her. "You're right. It's all so hazy." She skims the room, or as much of it as she can see from her position, jogging her memory. When her gaze lands on Mathilde, she blinks a few times and starts speaking. "I remember. We came here on a tour. I told you that. We came to the theatre to look around. The guide called for us to follow to the next room, but I lingered behind."

"Did you see something?" Harry asks.

"No, not at first. I simply wanted a break from the group. There was a pair of children, always talking so loudly. I wanted a moment to imagine the space without their chatter distracting me."

I hold back a laugh, knowing exactly what she means. Touring with H isn't much different.

"Martijn left with the others, so I was on my own. I noticed a splotch of colour on the ground near the autopsy table." Mrs Bakker stops and then corrects herself. "Right here, actually. I was coming down to see what it was. I thought someone from our group might have dropped something."

"It was my scarf," Harry interrupts, pointing towards the item Mathilde is holding.

"I was circling around the levels of the theatre and was nearly at the bottom when someone shoved me over the ledge."

"Did you see them?" Mathilde's eyes glitter with anger. I know how she feels.

"I... I can't remember." Mrs Bakker sniffles into her tissue, her emotions swamping her. She closes her eyes and goes silent, her brow furrowed in concentration.

None of us move. Even Harry freezes in place, her hand hovering an inch above Mrs Bakker's arm. We're all afraid to break the spell as Mrs Bakker searches her memories for any trace of the last moments before she was hit.

Finally, she flutters her lashes, coming back to the present. "I didn't see anyone. As far as I knew, I was all alone."

The students return with a tall older man in tow. As soon as he lays eyes on Mrs Bakker, he gives a cry and rushes to her side.

"Annegien!" He drops to his knees, his face devoid of colour as he takes in the sight of his wife lying on the floor.

Harry scoots to the side, allowing him to take her place in caring for his wife. The two converse quietly in Dutch as she explains what has happened.

The students approach me and Mathilde, as bewildered by the scene as we are.

The young man who spoke English earlier offers an update. "The medic should be here any minute. It takes them some time to get through the city, especially at this time of day. The guard is waiting to accompany them. Did the woman tell you what happened?"

"Someone shoved her from behind and she fell over the lowest balcony. Or, I should say, that's what she thinks happened. She was very shaky on the details."

The medics arrive then, a pair of middle-aged women who stride into the room, every movement a study of efficiency. They ignore our group of onlookers, going straight for Mrs Bakker. One checks her pulse while the other speaks in a clear tone, asking questions to assess her condition.

We stand in silence, not wanting to be distractions. We should leave them to their work, but no one wants to go until we're sure

Mrs Bakker will be okay. Finally, after some additional checks, the medics convince Mrs Bakker to take a quick trip to the A&E.

"You may have a cracked rib," the medic explains, her friendly smile and lilting accent putting both Mr and Mrs Bakker at ease. She uses her radio to call into the hospital to let them know they are on the way, and then she asks the rest of us to remain behind to speak with the security guard who will help them carry her down.

Mr Bakker thanks us all for coming to his wife's aid before leaving with the medics. Harry passes him her card with her mobile number scribbled on the back, and asks him to please let her know what the doctors say.

Giving a statement to the guard takes hardly any time. The students go first, explaining that they'd been working all afternoon and had barely left the room for anything other than the necessities. They hadn't known anything untoward had occurred until I burst into their office.

Mathilde, Harry, and I have little else to add. The theatre had been empty when we'd come in, and it was only by sheer chance we'd found Mrs Bakker. The guard gives us clearance to leave, his notepad painfully empty of facts. Try as I might, I can't think of anything else to tell him. Mathilde and I had been intent on our search for Harry, and in the crowded medicine hall, we hadn't heard anything unusual. Harry had been at the other end of the building and was on her way to search for her scarf when she heard me shout her name.

"Grazie, signore, for your help. Can I take a number where I can reach you in case we need to follow up on anything else?"

Harry produces another card and also provides Lavinia's name and number to the guard. With nothing else left to say, we leave him in the room, searching for an explanation for the extraordinary event.

Chapter Six

We exit the Palazzo del Bo in a much different frame of
mind than the one we had when we went in. My
footsteps are slow and my emotions in a state of turmoil as we
step onto the pavement in front of the building.

"There you are!" Kate's voice is tinged with exasperation when
she spots us. "I was about to send H in to search for you. Did all
three of you lose your way?"

"I don't think they got lost, Kate," H interrupts. "Iffen you
three were any paler, you'd be the same colour as the building."

I glance around, sure there must be some sign of disarray, but
the rest of the world is carrying on as if it were just another day. It
makes sense, in some ways. Only a few of us were there to witness
the event as it unfolded. From here, all looks placid.

Kate, however, recognises that H is speaking the truth. She
shifts her weight onto her heels, as if mentally steeling herself for
whatever we're about to tell her. "Did something happen to you?"

"Not to us," Harry rushes to reassure her. "Someone attacked
a woman inside Palazzo Bo. We found her lying insensible in the
anatomical theatre."

"Cosa?" Lavinia gasps, her hand flying up to her mouth. "Is she going to be okay?"

We shift over to stand out of the way of passing bicyclists and pedestrians, and slowly recount our misadventure inside the palazzo. Lavinia and Kate are both aghast, particularly when I get choked up telling them how we thought it was Harry at first.

"I feel so terrible," Mathilde bemoans. "If Nat and I had been a few minutes earlier, we might have prevented the attacker from acting. Or at least have glimpsed who it was."

"You can't blame yourself, Mathilde," Lavinia cuts in, holding out a hand to stave off Mathilde's next words. "It is impossible to have eyes everywhere. Unfortunately, that means crimes will happen without anyone to witness or stop them. Besides, it doesn't sound like any of you know why this woman was attacked. If you'd been in there on your own, it could have just as easily been one of you lying there instead." Lavinia stares at us, deep in thought, before finally coming to a conclusion. "I do not think you three are in the right place of mind to visit a restaurant this evening. Why don't you come to dinner at my house instead? I am sure I've got the ingredients for a nice pasta dinner."

"We don't want to put you to any trouble," Harry says politely.

"Please, it is no trouble. I had planned to invite you over one evening anyway, so this is simply a shifting of the schedule." Lavinia pulls out her mobile and sends off a short text to her husband to let him know of the change in plans. "Stefano can go to a friend's house to watch the football match and the kids can stay with my mother. Trust me, this is not a hardship for any of them."

Despite Lavinia's upbeat assurances, our mood is subdued as we begin the walk to Lavinia's home. She lives close enough to the centre that we don't need to take a taxi. Kate and Lavinia do their best to keep up a patter of conversation, while Mathilde, Harry, and I attempt to recover from our shock. H entertains himself by weaving between the passing pedestrians.

As we're walking under Padua's famed covered walkways, my mind returns to the scene in the anatomical theatre. My footsteps slow as I let the distance between myself and the others grow. I'm too upset to take part in a conversation.

Mathilde notices my absence and stops to wait for me. She doesn't need to ask what is weighing on my mind. "You're thinking about Mrs Bakker."

"Yes. I keep picturing that moment when we first spotted her. I was so convinced it was Harry."

"Me, too," Mathilde admits. "I could hear my heart pounding in my head as I looked down below me. My mind blanked, mostly because I didn't want to give words to what I was seeing. If you hadn't started shouting Harry's name, I think I might have passed out."

"Oh, Mathilde," I gasp and wrap an arm around her shoulders, hugging her. "We will not let Harry out of our sight, will we? She's certainly scared me enough already this trip, between the near tumble into traffic at the airport, and her fall down the stairs at the Basilica."

"She has certainly had a run of bad luck," Mathilde answers. "What's the old saying, that bad luck comes in threes? Hopefully, Harry's bad luck has run its course now."

I laugh and quietly agree with Mathilde, forcing a reassuring smile onto my face to cheer us both. But no matter how hard I try to seem okay, something about the events is still bothering me. Is it bad luck or could there be something more menacing afoot?

I'm still turning the idea over in my head when Harry says something to Kate and then slows down to join our little group.

"Kate and Lavinia started talking about the art world, so I told them I was coming back to check on the two of you." Harry pauses, taking a second to glance around us, making sure no one else is close enough to overhear her. "Nat and Mathilde, I know this might sound crazy, but I don't think Mrs Bakker getting hurt was an accident. I don't see any way she could have fallen over the balcony railing on her own."

Harry continues. "I've been thinking about my own troubles. It's possible I tripped when we were outside the airport, but I'm sure I felt someone shove me in the Basilica today. You two both said you thought I had been injured today at the Palazzo del Bo. What if it was supposed to be me?"

I open mouth to refute her logic, but nothing comes out. Our ever-practical Harry would be the last one to imagine someone is after her. "But who? And how?"

Harry grimaces. "An evil spirit? That's the only explanation I can find. A year ago, I'd have laughed at myself for even suggesting such a thing. But knowing what we do about the magical world, I can't discount the possibility."

"You think it might be an Eternal?" Mathilde twists her mouth to the side, testing the idea for merit. "Could they do that... I mean, before we create the connection?"

"There is one person we could ask," I point out. "H, can you come here?"

H scampers back to my side, flapping his wings as he leaps into my arms. "Oi, Nat, what do you need?"

"We've got a hypothetical question for you. In places outside of Oxford, where there isn't a strong magical connection, can the Eternals interact at all with the people?"

"I've 'eard other Eternals talkin' about this — those which 'ave ventured to other areas. It takes a lot of energy for them to get through. Just sayin' a single word or flickerin' into view would be a struggle." H narrows his eyes at me. "Why are you askin' this question?"

Instead of answering him, I probe for more information. "What about physically touching someone... or something?"

"Erm, I guess? They might do somethin' short and sharp, like move a single object. I'd 'ave to ask one of the wispie Eternals to be sure. Maybe Bartie or your grandda Alfred would know." H pushes out of my arms and flies in front of us so he can look me in the eye. "What's goin' on?"

Harry is the one to answer. "I think an Eternal might be behind my tumble at the Basilica and the attack on Mrs Bakker."

"An Eternal?" H lets out a nervous sneeze and somersaults through the air. Fortunately, the surrounding space is clear, and no one gets singed by his flames. He lands on his feet and screeches at us. "I knew I felt eyes on us when we were at the Basilica. But why would an Eternal want to 'urt you, 'Arry? Or anyone, for that matter?"

"That's the part where I'm stuck," she admits. But it is obvious from the determined set of her chin that she will not let the idea go.

With no better explanation at hand, I decide to explore the notion. "This isn't your first trip to Italy, right, Harry? Have you been to Padua before?"

"No," she answers, shaking her head. She waits until a Vespa rumbles past us before saying more. "Rob and I have visited a few times — Rome, Florence, Milan — but this is my first time here. And before you ask, no, I don't know anyone here, either."

"And you never had anything like this happen before?" Mathilde asks.

"No, nothing. The only place I've ever felt watched by an unseen presence is Oxford. And in that case, I now know I wasn't imagining things. It was St Margaret's Eternals keeping an eye on me."

We continue following Kate and Lavinia, passing through the streets of Padua without taking in any of the view. Mathilde, Harry, H, and I are too focused on searching for an explanation for the strange happenings.

Gradually, the shop displays are replaced by curtained apartment windows as the area becomes more residential. While we're fast approaching Lavinia's house, we're no closer to an answer.

I break the silence. "I hate to say this, but I think our only course of action right now is to wait and see what happens next."

Mathilde and Harry don't look happy with my suggestion, but neither argues. H, however, has another plan. He circles between us until he is walking close beside Harry.

"Don't worry, 'Arry. Until we can figure out who's after you, you can count on me to watch your back."

Lavinia stops outside an iron gate on a residential street. Every house sits tucked away behind concrete walls or iron fences lined with shrubs. Over the top of the walls, evergreen boughs climb into the air, providing shade in the summer and a natural defence against the rain in the autumn and spring. Green is, in fact, everywhere around us. From ivy trailing up the side of buildings, to rows of potted plants decorating the terraces, to the dense bushes shielding the houses from view.

Intrigued, Mathilde moves closer to Lavinia, angling around her to peer through the gate. "This feels like an entry to a secret garden."

"You're not far off," Lavinia admits, finally finding her keys in her handbag. "This part of the city is Città Giardino — garden city, in English. I grew up in this area, as did my husband Stefano. This is his family home, and my mother lives a few minutes' walk from here."

"I can't imagine living so close to my parents," Mathilde admits.

"Me either," I agree. "But there is something special about

living in a house that is passed down through the family. My fiancé and I are remodelling a house I inherited from my grandfather," I explain to Lavinia. "We still have a lot left to do, so I'm always on the lookout for inspiration."

"There's plenty to find here, Nat," Kate says, with a laugh. "Lavinia and Stefano have put their stamp on every square centimetre of this house. Wait until you see it."

"And now I wish I'd tidied up the kids' toys before I left this morning," Lavinia confesses, opening the gate with a flourish. "But a house is not a museum, I have to remind myself. There will be clutter, but that is to be expected with young children, no?"

"Absolutely," Harry reassures her. She winks as she adds, "It's Italian clutter, so even a mess will feel exotic."

The house sits within a nice-sized garden, dotted with shade trees. I spot a swing set in the back corner, with a tidy plant patch nearby. Although it is devoid of growth this late in the season, I can well imagine it providing a small supply of vegetables in the summer months.

The house is a terracotta colour, with lovely little terraces lining the front of the first and second floors. White wooden shutters frame each window, while blooming plants line the base of the terraces. It is picturesque and peaceful, and I immediately get a warm sense of home.

We follow Lavinia up a short flight of steps to enter the house through the main entrance. Inside, warm wooden floors and brightly painted walls make for a friendly atmosphere. Extravagant glass fixtures cast light from the ceiling, the whimsical floral designs reminding me of the Venetian adverts I saw posted on the walls of the airport.

"Make yourselves at home," Lavinia invites, pointing us towards the sitting room. Tall bookshelves line one wall, filled with books of every shape, size, and state. Some have worn bindings, making me think they've been passed down through the generations. Ceramic vases, porcelain figurines, and blown-glass sculptures break up the rows of books.

"May I?" Mathilde asks, but she doesn't wait for an answer before she strides over to the nearest bookshelf for a closer look, H close on her heels. I leave them to it, instead joining Kate and Harry as they take in a gallery wall of eclectic artwork.

The room carefully balances the old with the new. Antique end tables and lamps sit between modern furnishings which must have cost a small fortune. But it is the small touches of family life which prevent the room from feeling cold or austere. The reading glasses left abandoned on top of a book tell the story of a relaxing afternoon. There is a Barbie doll mixed in with the decorative figurines. Little handprints mar the perfect finish on the walls.

A cluster of framed photos sitting atop a wooden desk catches my eye. Nosy or not, I'd rather look at the pictures of people than stare at artwork. There are photos of Lavinia and a man who must be her husband, both smiling ear-to-ear on their wedding day. Her daughters are represented as well, starting with baby photos on to recent snapshots.

I scan the room, searching for more, and spot a collection of older picture frames on a nearby bookshelf. There are yellow-tinged photos of a much younger Lavinia, posing with her mother and grandmother. The family resemblance is clear. Further back, a photo is half-tucked away. Without a conscious thought, I reach out and retrieve it, bringing into the light of the room so I can see it more clearly.

The photo shows a trio of women standing together in a garden. They're all dressed to the nines, smiling brightly at whoever is behind the camera. It isn't their clothing, or their expressions, or even the setting which stops me in my tracks.

Standing next to a younger version of Lavinia's grandmother is a woman who looks remarkably like someone else I know.

"Harry!"

"What?" the woman herself replies from across the room.

"No, I wasn't calling you. It's this photo. Look at it — that woman is the spitting image of you!" I pass her the photo as she reaches my side.

She gasps in confirmation. "My word! If I didn't know there was no way this could be me, I would swear someone had photoshopped my face into the picture."

"You have a doppelganger!" Mathilde declares as she examines the photo. "That's so cool, Harry!"

"More like creepy," she mutters, looking very uncomfortable.

Kate comes over and takes the frame from Mathilde, and then motions for us to follow her. We troop through Lavinia's house as Kate guides us to the kitchen where Lavinia is preparing dinner.

"Did you need something?" Lavinia asks as we come in. "Maybe a glass of wine?"

"A glass of wine would be great, but that isn't why we've tracked you down. We couldn't help notice this photo." Kate passes Lavinia the silver frame, her expression deadly serious.

Lavinia gives Kate a strange look as she dries her hands, but she takes the photo and moves closer to the window so she can see it clearly. "This?" Her voice lilts upwards, making the single word into a question. "It's a photo of my nonna, her sister, and a friend of theirs." Lavinia glances up, searching Kate's face for an explanation. "What am I missing?"

Harry steadies her shoulders and steps forward, taking the picture frame back. She raises it close to her face and shifts until Lavinia has a clear view of the side-by-side. "Notice anything?"

Lavinia does as asked, flicking her gaze from the photo to Harry's face. I can see the moment the realisation hits her. She takes in a strangled breath and grabs the photo, peering intently at it. "You and my Zia Angelina could be gemelle! Twins!" she explains, in English.

"I didn't know your mother had a sister," Kate prods, drawing Lavinia's attention away from the photo.

"She's actually my prozia — my great aunt. She was my nonna's sister." Lavinia buffs the glass with her towel, clearing off the fingerprints. "I forgot I even had this photo. I should give it back to my nonna."

While the others seem somewhat satisfied by her response, there is one word which captures my attention. "Was? Is she dead?"

"Sí," Lavinia replies as she sets the photo safely aside on a nearby table. "She died in a house fire before I was born. It was a great tragedy for the family, as I'm sure you can imagine."

I can't stop myself from asking the next question. "A house fire? Was it an accident?"

"As far as I know..." Lavinia shrugs, thinking that will be the end of the discussion, but none of the rest of us move.

"I think we're going to need that wine now," Harry states, blinking rapidly at myself and Mathilde. I know exactly what she is trying to communicate. We'd been wondering why an Eternal in Italy would try to hurt Harry. Me finding that photo couldn't have been an accident.

As we divide up the remaining dinner preparation tasks and set the table, I'm compiling a list of questions in my head. What kind of person was Angelina? Is there any reason she could be out for vengeance? Or could there be another reason she is trying to get our attention?

I pointedly avoid thinking about the other alternative. What if Angelina's death wasn't an accident? Could whoever murdered her now be out to ensure Harry meets the same end?

Chapter Seven

Lavinia places abundant plates of steaming pasta and glasses of full-bodied red wine in front of each of us and invites us to enjoy our meal. Although the food is delicious and the conversation is friendly, my mind is elsewhere.

How do you tell someone that magic is real? No one had been there when Kate, Mathilde, and I made our discoveries. We'd each used a key to unlock our connection to Oxford's magic. We had felt a physical zing of electricity course through our bodies, and knew that something significant had shifted in our lives.

Before we'd come to Italy, we'd discussed who would be the best person to start our conversation with Lavinia. I'd argued for Kate, given their history together, but Kate and Mathilde had pushed for a different outcome. They thought it should be me.

I'm the only one with any experience of inducting an outsider into the world of magic. Harry had taken the news best, hardly batting an eye when I told her she was conversing with a ghost. Edward, my fiancé, had fainted when I gave him the news. And Trevor, a Detective Chief Inspector in Oxford and also Mathilde's significant other, had run terrified from the room.

Although Mathilde and Kate expressed full confidence in my

abilities, finding the right words to reveal our secret to someone else is no small task. It's no wonder I'm nervous. I take a sip of my wine to calm my nerves, but my throat is so dry that I end up choking on it instead. Harry, sitting beside me, reaches over to pat me on my back.

"Everything okay, Nat?" she asks.

I clear my throat twice and swallow a sip of water. "Yes, sorry about that. It went down the wrong way." I force myself to laugh it off, not wanting to worry Lavinia or anyone else. Just then, I feel a warm rush of air on my lower legs, followed by a heavy weight as H snuggles up against my legs under the table. His deep, soothing rumbles help take the edge off my nerves and give me the courage to proceed.

As my mind grows calm, I remember the notes I made before I left Oxford. I've planned the conversation in my mind. Now the only thing left to do is start it. Feeling better, I focus on finishing my dinner and enjoying the generous bowls of gelato accompanied by tiny amaretto biscuits and glasses of Vin Santo.

When our bowls are empty, a comfortable silence settles over the table. That is my cue to begin.

"Lavinia, I read a magazine article recently about ghostly appearances and strange happenings in Venice. Are there any stories about similar experiences here in Padua?"

Lavinia chuckles, clearly amused by my question. "You'd be hard-pressed to find a corner of Italy which doesn't have a story about ghosts, saints, miracles, or some other supernatural happening. Throughout our history, the deities have been leaving their mark on our people. Sometimes it's a curse, and others it is a blessing."

Pleased that she hasn't yet scoffed at the notion, I plod ahead. "Do people really believe those stories? Or is the tradition dying away with the older generations?"

She doesn't answer right away, instead giving the question

some consideration. "It is probably fairer to say that our willingness to believe grows as we age. My nonna is convinced she sees ghosts of prior generations. My daughters laugh and tell her she is imagining things. I can remember doing the same when I was little."

"But now?" I ask, urging her on.

Lavinia shrugs. "Perhaps it is wishful thinking, but as I get older, I find myself more drawn to the idea that my family might still remain here, watching over me. It could be the same with my nonna. She is ninety years old, and much of her generation has passed away. Believing that they are around, even if only in spirit form, brings her comfort. Who am I to deny her that?"

I sit up, preparing to ask my next question, but Kate jumps in before I can.

"Lavinia, what if your grandmother isn't wrong?" Kate doesn't wait for an answer. "What if there was a way for you, or me, or any of us here, to interact with people from the past?"

"Like a time machine? Or a ouija board?" Lavinia frowns, taken aback.

"No, not like that," Kate answers, shaking her head to stop Lavinia before she goes any further. "If you had the chance to speak with a historical figure, right here and now — to touch them, talk to them, learn from them — would you want to do it?"

"Who wouldn't?" Lavinia quips, still not grasping Kate's seriousness. "Isn't that every history student's dream?"

As Kate settles back in her chair, looking relieved by Lavinia's response, I move to the next step in my plan.

I begin with a concise explanation. "Four centuries ago, two famed researchers at Oxford stumbled across a way to make that seemingly impossible dream into a reality. Since then, caretakers have kept a close watch over this secret, handing it down through the family line. I know this because I am one of them. So is Mathilde," I say, pointing to my right where Mathilde is seated.

"And I am one, Lavinia," Kate adds. She crosses her hands in her laps and waits expectantly for Lavinia to react. Lavinia returns her gaze without saying a word. I can tell from her wide-eyed expression that she hasn't understood the significance of what we've shared with her. More than anything, she looks confused as she glances between us, waiting for someone to spell it out for her.

Good thing I have one other trick up my sleeve. It is my fallback, and one which has served me well before.

I scoot back my chair and pat my lap, inviting H to leap into it. I try not to grimace as his talons scrape my legs and his wing nearly whacks me in the face. With a minimum of shifting around, I get him comfortably settled.

Seated across from me, Lavinia raises an eyebrow at my unorthodox decision to invite my cat to join us at her dinner table. Little does she know, it will only get stranger from here.

"Lavinia, I know you don't know me very well," I begin, "but I need to ask you to do something that is going to sound decidedly odd. I'm going to reach my hand across the table. Could you grasp it?"

She doesn't act straight away, only doing so when Kate nudges her with her elbow. "Go on, Lavinia. It will all become clear in a moment."

"I hope it will become clear," I clarify. "In truth, I'm not one hundred per cent sure this will work, but we have to try." With my free hand, I push my plate to the side and make space for H to join us. "Lavinia, with your other hand, please reach over and hold on to one of H's paws."

Lavinia blinks rapidly, so far into the unknown at this point that she can do nothing other than to go along with it. She gasps softly when H offers her a hand without me needing to say a word of instruction. When Lavinia's connection with me and H is complete, I lay my other hand upon H's head. I can't stop the smile from bursting across my face when I feel the zing of energy leap from H to me, and then down my arm into Lavinia's hand.

Lavinia shivers as the magical current runs across her shoulders and back down to H's paw. She lets loose an exclamation in Italian when H's seemingly furry paw turns into a scaly hand complete with sharp talons.

"Don't be scared," Kate murmurs, patting Lavinia's arm. "Magic is real, my friend. H is a wyvern. He began his life as a gargoyle carved into Oxford's Bodleian Library. Ghosts are real as well. They walk among us, whispering guidance into our ears. We call these magical people and creatures the Eternals."

I don't dare move. None of us do, as Lavinia processes the scene in front of her and Kate's explanation. She raises a hand to her mouth and inhales deeply through her nose, before swallowing loud enough for us to hear. When she opens her mouth, I don't know what to expect her to say.

But it isn't to me she looks first. Instead, she turns to Kate, her longtime friend. Kate, who has seen her through good times and bad, and is certainly someone she can trust.

"Dimmi, Kate. Tell me the truth. Tell me everything."

Kate starts her tale of discovering the magic of Oxford at the beginning. Mathilde, Harry, and I are as enraptured as Lavinia is. With everything that has happened over the past year, we never had time to compare our experiences. Kate's and Mathilde's weren't wildly different, as both were initiated by my predecessor Lillian. I can't help but smile as I think back on that fateful day when I picked up an old-fashioned key and turned it in a lock, and moments later found myself staring down at a walking, talking, and fire-breathing wyvern.

The bottle of wine runs dry and we all switch to glasses of sparkling water as the conversation turns serious.

"Oxford's magical connection has been a carefully guarded secret for centuries. The original discoverers had a good reason for keeping quiet about it. We saw ourselves what could happen if access fell into the wrong hands," Kate explains, after telling the story of last year's adventure.

"I understand," Lavinia replies with a solemn look on her face. "You are placing an incredible trust in me. I am honoured."

"It is a responsibility that we all share," I add, reaching across the table to give her hand a squeeze. "Having access to centuries' worth of history and expertise is invaluable, which is why we feel it is so important that we create magical connections in other places. I hope you will see it as a gift, just as we do."

"A priceless gift," Lavinia agrees. She motions towards H, who is curled in a ball and is sleeping on the top of the table, worn out from the day's excitement. "Now tell me more about these Eternals of yours. Will I get a wyvern of my own?"

"I can say confidently that H is one of a kind. But you will no doubt find other magical creatures living in Padua once we establish a solid connection. In fact, we encountered a few today."

"A few?" Kate arches an eyebrow.

"So much has happened. I didn't have a chance to update you," I explain, my tone apologetic. "I'll start with the positive experiences, if that's okay." I show Lavinia the collar hanging around H's neck. "The Eternals helped us create a mobile connection to Oxford's magic, one which allows H to accompany us on our trips. What none of us realised, however, is just how far H's connection extends. This afternoon, he leapt into the lap of the statue of Elena Cornaro at Palazzo del Bo, and for a moment, we could communicate with her. The same thing happened again with the lions outside the cafe."

"The lions at Caffé Pedrocchi?" Lavinia asks, her eyes wide in shock.

"They seemed friendly enough," I rush to reassure her. "The connection is very unstable. All they could manage was a flip of their tails to send H flying between them."

Lavinia sits back in her chair, marvelling at my words. "First a wyvern. Now you're telling me I'll get to speak with Elena Cornaro and play with stone lions?"

"That's only the beginning," Kate says with a laugh. "Nat's grandfather is an Eternal. I wouldn't be surprised if you get a chance to meet someone from your family tree."

"Aren't you forgetting someone?" Mathilde asks, looking pointedly at Kate. When Kate wrinkles her brow in confusion, Mathilde adds, "Bartie. Your partner?"

"Aspetta! Bartie — your Bartie — is an Eternal?" Lavinia is well and truly shocked. "You're dating a ghost?"

"Not a ghost," Kate corrects her. "Well, not in the way you're imagining, Vinia. Oxford has a powerful connection to the magical field. Because I am a prefect, Bartie is as solid and real as any other person I'd meet on the street."

"That explains why I haven't met him yet."

Kate shrugs. "Yes, our ability to socialise with others is hampered, but we make it work. And should all go well with our attempt to create a permanent magical connection here in Padua, Bartie will come for a visit."

We fall quiet in time to hear a man's voice echo from the front hallway. Lavinia calls for her husband Stefano to come and say hello. He is a little older than he appeared in the photo I'd seen earlier. But his ready smile and affable nature is immediately obvious as he makes his way around the table, shaking our hands as he introduces himself. He barely raises an eyebrow at H's slumbering form, taking the sight of a cat on his dinner table in stride.

After Stefano heads upstairs to bed, we lend a hand to clear the table and wash the dishes. When all is in order, we return to the more comfortable sitting room, with warm mugs of tea in our hands.

Lavinia looks my way. "While we were washing up, I remembered something you said earlier, Nat... about your experience with Padova's Eternals. You said you'd start with the positive. That implies there must also be a negative."

I nudge H, making sure he is awake. We all need to pay attention to this part of the conversation. "It's about Harry," I explain. "We think someone is targeting her. An Eternal," I add.

"Harry?" Lavinia looks at the woman in question and Harry nods back in confirmation. "Your fall today in the Basilica. That wasn't an accident?"

"No, someone shoved me while I was standing at the top of the stairs."

"Not only that," I interrupt. "The woman who was attacked at the Palazzo looked similar to Harry. Very similar," I stress. "When Mathilde and I first spotted her, we both thought it was Harry." My throat closes tight, preventing me from saying anything else.

"That must have been awful," Lavinia says as I dash away a tear. She pauses, gathering her thoughts. "What could an Italian Eternal have against Harry?"

"I don't think I'm the real target. I think it has something to do with your great-aunt Angelina," Harry explains, giving me a moment to calm down. "That's our working hypothesis, anyway. You said yourself that we looked like twins. When you put me, someone who looks just like Angelina, together with a member of your family, we've got all the right pieces for a case of mistaken identity."

Mathilde coughs, capturing our attention. Her mouth turns down in a frown. "Or it could be the ghost of Angelina herself."

"Zia Angelina? Attacking an innocent woman?" Lavinia shakes

her head. "From everything I know about her, that would be very out of character."

"Why don't you tell us about her," Kate suggests. "You said she died before you were born."

"Yes, she did. She and my nonna were incredibly close, and my nonna told me many stories of her as I was growing up." Lavinia's eyes get a faraway look. "My mamma idolised her, and I used to imagine she was watching over me."

"Maybe she was," Harry reminds her.

"That's a lovely thought," Lavinia agrees. "Let me tell you what I know."

Most of what Lavinia remembers are stories of moments from Angelina's life. She paints a picture of a self-assured woman who wasn't afraid to make her own way in the world.

"She married young, as was traditional back then," Lavinia explains. "Her husband died suddenly before they had children. She never married again. In part, it was her way of honouring him. But I think she also enjoyed the freedom which came from being a widow. She would dress up and go to the opera and the museum openings, or go travelling around Europe. She was very independent."

Kate leans over and picks up the framed picture from the nearby end table. "I can see why your mother would have idolised her. She must have seemed very exotic compared to your nonna."

Lavinia chuckles. "My mother got into trouble more than once for playing dress-up in Angelina's clothing and jewellery. Some of her things are still in storage at my nonna's house. Not everything was lost in the fire," she hastens to add.

"Do you know much about how she died?" Harry quizzes, gently nudging the conversation forward.

"I looked it up in the newspaper archives when I was younger," Lavinia confesses. "I was curious, but I didn't want to upset my mamma or my nonna. It's been a long time, but from what I recall, they thought it was an accident. Something with the gas or electricity. One end of the house was destroyed."

"Hmm," Harry mutters, pondering Lavinia's words. "That is certainly tragic, but I'm not sure how much it helps us. Based on what you know, do you think it is at all possible that it wasn't an accident?"

Lavinia gives an artful shrug in reply as she nibbles her lower lip. "There's a wyvern sitting in my home, and you tell me ghosts are real. At this point, I believe anything is possible."

I barely suppress a laugh.

Sitting up in a rush, Lavinia suggests, "Could we ask Angelina? What if she is an Eternal?"

It's a good question, and I wish I had a better response for her. "If we had a strong connection to the magical field, I'd say it was certainly worth a try. But here... our ability to communicate is so weak. We'd never manage a long enough conversation with anyone to find out if she is even around. I wouldn't want to attempt a permanent connection until we know it is safe to do so."

Lavinia sits back, her eyes looking sideways, still deep in thought. "What if we knew exactly where to find her?" That gets all our attention. "My nonna is convinced she sees Angelina's ghost. Before tonight, I wrote it off as wishful thinking, but now I'm not so sure."

"You think Angelina follows your grandmother around?" Kate taps her chin, considering the idea.

"Not all the time," Lavinia corrects her. "Nonna still says mass for her each year, on the anniversary of her death. Once a month, she visits Angelina's grave, always on her own. She says it brings her peace to go there. Nonna talks to Angelina, updating her on the family and their friends. She is sure Angelina is there listening."

I glance around the room, measuring the reactions of the

others. Mathilde, Harry, and Kate all look determined. Our next step is clear. "It sounds like we've got a location. But we'll need a careful plan before we go there. Until we know what's going on, we're not taking any chances with Harry's safety."

Chapter Eight

We take the night to sleep on the idea before we make any plans on how we might attempt to contact Angelina. Sheer exhaustion caused by our long day of walking around Padua ensures I fall asleep easily, but my rest is far from peaceful. Nightmare visions of Harry lying dead, bleeding, or otherwise injured chase through my dreams. I toss and turn in the strange bed.

H hears me cry out in my sleep and slips into my room to check on me. Sensing my need for comfort, he curls up by my feet, his body radiating warmth. Finally, I drift off into a dreamless void.

After several restorative cups of coffee and some toast, I'm feeling somewhat more like myself. The one upside to my restless night is my newfound conviction that we must see this through.

When everyone is dressed and ready to face the day, we regroup in the sitting room of our holiday flat. Lavinia has joined us. I watch her carefully as she comes into the room. Her eyes search the space, not stopping until her gaze lands on H. I know that expression of relief all too well. It is one thing to be told magic is real when night has fallen and all seems possible. It is quite another to see a wyvern lounging on a sofa in broad daylight.

I pull a pair of extra chairs into the room, making space for all of us to sit comfortably. Harry, Mathilde, and H are on the sofa. Lavinia chooses an armchair, leaving Kate and me to sit in the chairs from the kitchen table. As the de facto planner in our group, all heads turn my way.

I take a moment to glance at my scribble-filled notepad, as much to refresh my memory as to find the best place to start. Our task is not without danger. But now isn't the time for my courage to fail.

I address the room. "Let's start with what we know. An unidentified Italian Eternal has fixated on Harry, and our best guess is that this is a case of mistaken identity. I have outlined several options for consideration. Before I get into them, I'd like to say upfront that I don't think all of them are viable. However, I thought it appropriate to at least raise them with you to ensure we agree. Is that acceptable?"

Harry answers me. "Yes, Nat. That sounds logical. I think it is important that we not rush to judgement, particularly since it is my safety at risk."

"Very well, I'll begin. The simplest solution would be to send you home, Harry." I pause and raise a hand, preventing Harry from interrupting me with her expected refusal to walk away. "I say simplest, but not necessarily safest. We know the ghostly Eternals can travel, but their strength and ability to interact with the living varies greatly depending on the strength of the connection between Earth and the magical field. There is nothing to stop this Eternal from following Harry back to Oxford, where the magic would make them as dangerous as any living being."

"At least here, we have some modicum of control over what they can do," Mathilde agrees. "As we've seen, they can strike out, but little more than that. Now that we are aware of the problem, we can protect Harry from most harm. No walking along balconies or ledges," she adds, wagging a finger at Harry.

"You don't need to tell me," Harry says with a laugh. "Even if the Eternals couldn't travel, I wouldn't feel right leaving. As we saw with Mrs Bakker, anyone who remotely resembles Angelina is at risk of being hurt. We are the only ones who might identify the culprit and see them stopped. What kind of prefects would you be if you ran scared, leaving an Eternal here to harm others?"

"We are not the type of people to turn tail at the first hint of danger," I reply. "That leads me nicely to my second point. If we aren't leaving, we should continue with our original plan. We came to Padua intending to create a new connection to the magical field around the Earth. I still believe this is the right thing to do. However, before we attempt making any sort of permanent connection, we need to resolve this situation."

Mathilde waves a hand to stop me. "Wait a minute, Nat. While I agree with everything you've said so far, I don't see how we can possibly figure out what is going on without some kind of help from the Eternals in Padua. We're making a lot of educated guesses, but they're still far from confirmed."

"We're in a catch-22 situation," Kate grumbles. "We can't risk using the magic, but also can't make any progress without it."

"You're right, Kate. I've been thinking about that exact problem. As luck would have it, we may have stumbled across a solution last night at dinner. Remember when Lavinia's husband Stefano came in to meet us? He barely noticed that H was curled up in the middle of the table."

"He didn't? I was so caught up in our discussion, I didn't even think about H still being sat there," Mathilde replies, her eyes sparkling with curiosity.

"I didn't think much of it at the time either, but when I saw H curled up on my bed this morning, the image jiggled a thought loose in my mind. I realised H has been passing without comment every time he's stuck to the middle of our group. The only times someone has noticed something odd about his behaviour is when he has been far away from us, like in the airport security checkpoint." I turn to H. "What do you think?"

"I 'adn't thought about it, but you're right. I certainly feel more confident when I'm walkin' in between you four." H gives me a smokey snort of approval. "Way to use your loaf, Nat!"

"Okay... so H's connection grows stronger when we circle him. How does that help?" Harry asks. "Are you suggesting we stand around H and hold hands, and then call for Angelina?"

I can tell by Harry's expression that she thinks I've lost the plot, but I plough ahead anyway. "I know it sounds odd, but logically, I think it is our best chance for success. H has a connection to the magical field. Lavinia has a connection to Angelina. If the two stand together beside Angelina's grave, a location which has a clear connection with the Eternal we want to contact, there's a good chance she will hear them and respond. The hard part will be stabilising the connection long enough for us to find out whether the fire was an accident."

Motioning to Harry, Mathilde, and Kate, I explain, "That's where the four of us come in. We need to strengthen and focus the connection. We can do that by forming a circle around them."

A hush falls when I finish my explanation. All around me, I see faces deep in thought as my friends consider my plan. It sounds outlandish when I say it aloud, but inside, I know it has merit. After all, Sir Christopher Wren did something very similar when he first stumbled across the existence of magic. Until now, we've had it easy. Magic exists, ghosts are real, and we prefects can speak with them whenever we want. Here in Italy, it is as though we've travelled back in time to the early days of magical exploration. We'll need to keep an open mind if we want any chance of success.

Kate sits back in her chair, her face carefully blank of all expressions. "As crazy as it sounds, I can't fault your logic. Given our time constraints and the risk that someone else will get hurt, I doubt we'll come up with any better plan. However," she adds, turning her gaze to Lavinia, "I think Harry and Lavinia should have the final say on whether we go forward."

"I agree," Mathilde chimes in. "And don't forget about H."

H agrees readily enough. "I'll do it. That's why I'm 'ere, remember? Iffen there's anything I can do, you can count on me to lend a 'and."

"The same holds true for me," Harry adds, then her voice softens as she turns to Lavinia. "I wouldn't want you to feel you're under any obligation, dear. Twenty-four hours ago, you thought H was a cat and magic was fiction. If you aren't ready, or if this is too much, too quickly, we'll put our heads together and see if there is any alternative solution which wouldn't put you in the hot seat."

I keep a close watch on Lavinia, searching for signs of her true feelings. If she is truly right for the role of prefect, I have no doubts she will say yes.

She takes a deep breath and releases it slowly before finally speaking. "Family is everything for us Italians. If Angelina's death was not an accident, I couldn't live with myself if I knew I'd turned my back on an opportunity to seek justice on her behalf. That said, I am also a mother and a wife. We hope to connect with Angelina. But we might attract the attention of whomever is responsible for the attacks on Harry and Mrs Bakker. So I must ask for your help in keeping me safe while we do this."

Kate stretches out a hand and pats Lavinia's arm. "We have faced far worse, and come out safely on the other side. H may look small, but his spirit is fierce, and I can think of no one better to protect us all."

"Then we agree," Harry declares. "Nat and I have university meetings with the Padua delegation this afternoon. I know it isn't ideal, but can we get access to the cemetery after dark?"

Lavinia promises to request a key to the gates. I add the assignment to my plan and then flip the page of my notebook over to reveal a clean one underneath. "I suggest we focus our efforts now on drafting a list of questions for Angelina. We don't know how long we'll be able to speak with her, so it would behoove us to be efficient with our words."

I tap my pen against my lips, organising my thoughts before I put pen to paper. The morning flies by as we discuss options and firm up our plans. I'm in my element as I diagram the layout of the cemetery and mark our places for where we can all stand.

When Harry and I have to take our leave to attend a meeting to discuss the twinning ceremony, I reluctantly hand responsibility for note-taking over to Mathilde. "I won't ask you to document as much detail as I would, but can you at least make note of the high points of the plan?"

"I'll do my best," she promises in a serious voice, but I catch the cheeky wink she makes when she thinks I'm not looking. I don't bother to chastise her. I'm all too accustomed to my friends making light of my reams of charts, graphs, and lists.

Halfway out the door, I come to a halt when a thought crosses my mind. I bid Harry to wait and make a quick dash back into the front room.

"H!" I call, interrupting the group's discussion. "Would you mind meeting me at the Palazzo del Bo later this afternoon? I've got an idea and your help will be critical to executing it."

"I can't say no when you put it that way, now can I?" the little wyvern agrees. He holds his head high, clearly proud of his central role in my plans. "What time should I meet you, missie?"

"I'll text Mathilde when my meeting wraps up. And on that note, I'd better run." With a quick wave goodbye, Harry and I head on our way.

❖

After an interminably long ceremonies meeting, with plenty of opinions and little appetite for compromise, Harry and I finally emerge into the late afternoon sunlight and fresh air.

Harry sighs in relief. "My word, Nat. I don't know how you do it. I've sat through my fair share of meetings in my career, but this one ranks near the top of the most frustrating ones."

"At least we had fair warning before we went in. Asking the Eternals for advice on Italian business culture was the best prep work I did. I'd already set it in my mind that today's meeting would yield lots of talking and few results." I wrap my arm through Harry's and guide her towards a nearby cafe. "Come on, I'll treat you to a hot chocolate while we wait for H to join us."

One incredibly thick and rich cup of dark chocolate later, H swoops from the sky to land on top of our outdoor table for two. Without a word of greeting, I pop the top off a takeaway cup and slide it over to H.

"I'll take a 'ot chockie over a 'ello any day, Nat," he grunts before upending the cup and pouring the hot drink down his throat. He finishes it with a smacking sound and a quick hiss of flames to eliminate any remaining traces of chocolate stains from his snout.

Harry and I exchange amused glances as we gather our things and prepare to leave.

"Now that you've been properly rewarded for your flight over, I need your help with a task," I state. "We're going to send Angelina an invitation to join us this evening."

"An invitation?" Harry scrunches her brow, weighing my idea. "How will we do that? And where does the Palazzo del Bo fit into it? I'm not keen to return there after what happened yesterday."

"That's understandable, Harry." I pat her arm reassuringly. "But unfortunately, the only Eternal we know in Padua has a seat of honour in the Palazzo."

"Elena Cornaro?" H asks, his eyes lighting up.

"That's the one! We'll have to talk fast, but do you think it's worth a try to see if we can use her to send a message to Angelina? Lavinia said her aunt studied at the university, so I'm hoping Elena will know who she is."

"It certainly can't hurt to make the effort," Harry agrees. She squares her shoulders and leads our trio towards the arched entrance to the Palazzo courtyard. Our visit only takes a few minutes.

"Light her up, H," I order.

H inhales deeply, sending a roiling wave of magical flames licking over the marble statue of the famous Italian female scholar. As soon as her stone eyes blink, I blurt out my request. She barely has time to nod her agreement before our connection falters and she once again turns into unyielding stone.

Our task complete, Harry, H, and I rush to our rental flat, where we find Mathilde and Kate waiting for us. Our conversations are subdued as we eat a quick dinner. No one has much of an appetite. We're too nervous about what might happen later in the evening.

As I pick at my food, my mind swirls with images of a graveyard, dark with shadows. Headstones jut from the ground, their carvings long since faded with time. Spiders skitter over the ground, weaving silken webs in between the bare branches of the trees. I can almost hear the hoot of a lone owl and the brush of leaves on the ground as we weave between the final resting places of Padua's dead.

I lean over and whisper to Mathilde, "I wish we didn't have to go out after dark."

"Me, too," she agrees with a shiver. "But time is of the essence."

H looks up from his bowl of cheesy pasta. "Don't you worry, missies. I'll keep you safe. All of you."

Thus reassured, we make quick work of tidying the kitchen

and then shrug on our coats. Harry doles out scarves, gloves, and torches, and with no small amount of trepidation, we leave for the cemetery.

We walk in a tightly packed group, with Lavinia and Kate up front, Harry safely in the middle, and Mathilde and I behind. H flies over our heads, sending jets of flame in warning to any Eternal who might dare to come near.

Every noise makes me jump — a car horn, the roar of a motorcycle, even a child's squeal. My imagination runs wild, turning every city noise into the shrieks of an enraged Eternal. By the time we reach the gates of the graveyard, my nerves are frayed.

Harry, however, is stoic. Her chin is firm, her gaze unwavering. If she can be so brave in the face of a threat, I can do no less. I force oxygen into my lungs and regulate my breathing until my heartbeat slows to a normal tempo.

Lavinia slides a key into the padlock holding the gates closed. The lock pops open with an audible click, followed by an earsplitting screech as the gate swings wide. Mathilde grabs my arm, far from her normal relaxed self, and scoots against my side. Together, we step closer to Harry, crowding her from behind as Lavinia hesitates at the cemetery entrance. Our group is packed so tightly I can hear Lavinia whispering to herself in Italian.

"What's wrong, Lavinia?" Kate asks, glancing at her in concern.

"It's nothing..." Lavinia shakes her shoulders and stands straighter. "I'm sure it's all in my imagination."

"No, I feel it too," Harry says, her head whipping left and right, looking around nervously.

Not wanting to take any chances, I wave my arm to attract H's attention. He circles overhead and swoops down to land at my feet.

"I don't like this place," he announces without preamble.

"Every time I fly over the gate, I can 'ear faint voices shoutin' at us. Are you sure you want to go inside?"

"We don't have any other choice, H," I remind him. "Would you mind flying a lap over the grounds to check the lay of the land ahead of us?"

"Nothin' will get past me, missies. Iffen you 'ear me 'ollerin' at you, run. Don't stop to ask questions, okay?" H takes flight, spewing warning smoke as he bravely flies ahead.

Inside the gate, a pebbled pathway stretches before us, the rocks gleaming in the pale moonlight, in stark contrast to the shadowed grounds. Marble and stone grave markers are poised like soldiers in the darkness, standing watch over their inhabitant's final resting place. I struggle to contain the flights of fancy that send shivers along my spine, but the spooky nature of our surroundings is too powerful to overcome.

Further ahead, a great cloud of shooting flames flashes across the sky. We freeze, not daring even to breathe as we wait for word from H.

"Zia Angelina's tomb is that way," Lavinia confesses, her voice grim. "Should we turn back?"

"No," I rush to reply. "If the situation was dangerous, H would give us warning. He may be using his flames to strengthen Angelina's connection, assuming she got our message and is there waiting." I motion for Kate to swap places with me and move into the lead, urging the others onward. "We should hurry."

I walk as fast as I can without resorting to running, my long strides eating up the ground as I follow the path through the cemetery. There is no way to hide our footsteps, each tread crunching on the loose pebbles. I put my complete faith in our magical wyvern. He would never allow anything to happen to us, and he has more than one trick up his proverbial sleeve, not the least being the ability to assume a gigantic form.

The path twists to the right, bringing a stone marker topped with a waist-high carved cherub into view. Without Lavinia saying a word, I know it must belong to Angelina. H hovers above the ground, his flames illuminating an otherworldly feminine shape. She flickers in and out of view in time with H's exhalations as she paces the length of her grave.

"Zia Angelina?" Lavinia calls loudly, her voice heavy with incredulity. "Sei tu?"

The ghostly woman spins around to face us. She looks so much like Harry that I gasp in surprise. Seeing the photo was one thing, but coming face-to-face with a spirit version of my close friend is an entirely new experience, and not one which I wish to repeat.

Angelina's eyes are wide with fear. With her hands out front, she implores us to stop where we are. Although she is clearly shouting, we can only catch a few words here and there.

"You mustn't be..." Angelina warns, before her voice goes silent. Seconds later, we hear her again. "Not safe!"

I grab Lavinia's arm to prevent her from rushing over to her aunt. Although Angelina's warning shows she is not the one behind the attacks on Harry, I'm still wary of getting too near, especially while she is so upset. Harry moves to Lavinia's side and nudges me move forward.

Taking a half-step ahead of the others, I hold my hands out front and plead with Angelina to calm down. "We know Harry is at risk. That's why we're here. We need your help. But you must settle down or we'll never manage to solidify a connection to the magical field."

Ghostly Angelina shakes her head furiously at me. "Too strong... must run.."

I switch my attention to H, silently asking him for help. He halts his flames, his wings batting hard enough to send drafts of wind through the air. His powerful strokes shift him until he is positioned between us and Angelina.

He drifts forwards until he is nearly nose to nose with Angelina. "Listen, wispy! The missies 'ere know 'ow to stop whoever it is, but you've got to lend a 'and."

Angelina leans sideways to see past H, checking for confirmation.

I give a quick nod of reassurance. "We know how to make a temporary connection..." I trail off when she waves for me to stop. Sensing her need to communicate, H inhales deeply and shoots out another rush of flames.

"Il fuoco! The fire... No accident..." Angelina says more, but her franticness is making the connection too unstable to even allow for lipreading.

"We guessed as much," I interject. "Do you know who it was?"

We all collectively exhale when she gives a nod of affirmation. We're so close to getting an answer, none of us move.

"Chi é stato?" Lavinia asks in a hoarse shout.

Illuminated in a fresh outpouring of magical flames, just as Angelina opens her mouth to answer, an icy wind sweeps across the grounds to our right, gathering a flurry of dried leaves and sticks into a swirling mass.

The dark cloud of dead foliage boils larger until it is roughly the size and shape of a person. Almost as one, Angelina and H leap into action. H rears back, gathering height before diving straight for our unearthly attacker.

Angelina uses her remaining energy to protect us. She spares barely more than a second to give us a final shout before throwing herself into the path of the oncoming whirlwind.

As soon as she passes beyond the border of her grave, she disappears from sight. Between H's dive and Angelina's lunge, the dust and rubbish cloud explodes, sending tiny pieces of debris showering over us.

I throw an arm over my face, protecting my mouth and eyes from the flying bits of dirt and leaves. It takes a moment for the wind to die down. I spin around, frantic to check on the others. They're huddled together, with Lavinia and Harry in the front, leaves sticking to their hair and coats. Otherwise, however, they appear to be unharmed.

H lands at my feet and uses his fiery breath to clean the dust from his scales.

"Is everyone okay?" I ask while dusting myself off.

"Nothing a shower can't fix," Harry reassures me. Although I imagine she is as shaken as I am, Harry is not the type to allow some dirt and leaves to ruffle her feathers. Her no-nonsense tone instils the others with a much-needed sense of calm. "I think whoever that was is gone now. Look, even the clouds have cleared."

We gaze upwards at the half moon, now visible thanks to a gap in the cloudy sky. The weighty feeling of danger has disappeared, leaving behind the crisp night air and a faint smell of smoke left from H's flames.

H marches along the path, his snout held high as he sniffs. "You're safe enough now, Nat. But I wouldn't linger, iffen I were you."

"No worries on that point," I reassure him. "Before we go, did anyone catch Angelina's last words?"

Lavinia is rooted to the spot, her attention firmly fixed on her aunt's grave. At my question, she gives herself a quick shake and looks my way. "I heard her, Nat. She shouted something in Italian, but I didn't catch it all. Everything happened too fast."

Kate wraps an arm over Lavinia's shoulder, slowly turning her away from the grave. "Whatever you caught is more than the rest of us. Tell us what you remember. Hopefully, it will be enough to get us started."

Lavinia blinks a few times and stares off into the distance, searching her memory. "The words don't make much sense on their own, but given they're all we've got, I'll tell you what I heard. She said something about making her choice, and then ended with the words *together forever*."

"That's ominous-sounding," Mathilde says in a grim voice. "But it isn't the only piece of information we got. She mentioned the fire, and I don't think she meant H's flames. What else could she have referred to than the cause of her death? She clearly knew the identity of her killer. That effectively rules out a stranger."

"Then that is where we will start. Is everyone still up for the challenge?" I ask, checking my friends for agreement. While Lavinia is still shaken, Harry, Kate, and Mathilde wear matching expressions of determination. "Let's get out of here and go someplace warm where we can plan our next steps."

We retrace our steps in silence, giving me time to think about the task before us — a fifty-year-old cold case to solve so we can stop an Eternal with a penchant for violence. I slide into step beside Mathilde and link my arm through hers. Our lives as magical prefects will never be boring.

Chapter Nine

Not wanting to disturb Lavinia's family, we beat a hasty retreat to our rental flat in the centre of Padua. The sitting room is barely large enough to accommodate all of us, but we make it work. I take one look at Lavinia's shivering form and disappear into the kitchen to prepare steaming cups of tea.

"Grazie tanto," Lavinia moans as she wraps her fingers around the hot surface of the ceramic mug I pass her. The smell of mint rises from the pale amber liquid, soothing the rough edges of her nerves.

It takes a couple more trips to distribute mugs of tea to the rest of the group. H scoffs down a stale croissant leftover from breakfast and then takes a seat in the front window. He makes no bones about what he is doing. His gaze is fixed on the street out front, keeping a careful watch out for any signs of the murderous Eternal we encountered in the graveyard.

Matilde pats the cushion next to her on the sofa and I slide into the space. Over the rim of my mug, I let my gaze skip around the room, taking in the women around me. Harry is my top concern. I needn't have worried. She sits up straight in her chair, undaunted by the scare we just had. Older than the rest of us, she's experienced her share of scrapes and challenges, and knows well that melting down won't help.

I catch Kate's eye as she does the same thing. She raises her eyebrows, silently asking if I'm okay. I reply with a reassuring smile and a single nod. It's enough for her. Out of the corner of my eye, I catch Mathilde give a similar reply when Kate's gaze moves on.

The remaining person is the one who has us all concerned. Lavinia stares into her mug, lost in thought. Kate taps her on the arm to bring her back to the present.

"How are you doing with all of this? If you want out, no one will judge you."

Lavinia shakes her head, sending her light brown hair tumbling over her shoulders. "No, Kate. I don't want to back out now. That scene in the graveyard terrified me, but I could see you were equally shocked."

"We've had our own troubles. I won't lie. But moments like tonight are the rare exception."

"As awful as it was to have someone try to attack us, it shored up my decision to stay involved. If whoever that was hoped to scare me away, they are in for a surprise. There's no way I can rest now that I know my zia was murdered!"

"Us either," Harry chimes in from her seat across the room. She's tucked into an armchair near the bookshelf. Her eyes flash a warning to back up her words. Harry is fully invested in solving this crime, and not only because her own life is at risk.

Kate rubs her arms, still warming herself after the chilling events.

Mathilde sets her mug on the coffee table and wipes her palms on her trousers. She wiggles on the sofa as she struggles with something.

I elbow her. "Out with it, Mathilde. What's got you so worried?"

Mathilde huffs a breath and turns her head to the side so she can look me in the face. "I agree with the rest of you, and I know walking away isn't an option. But, are we really going to do this... solve a cold case, I mean? None of us are detectives."

"After all the mysteries we've solved in Oxford, I feel like we've at least earned an honorary badge," I reply in a joking tone. "That said, you raise a fair point. It's one thing for us to say we want to figure out who killed Angelina. It's another to do it. And that's before we consider the fact that we're far from home."

Harry chimes in, "We've got a limited window of time here in Padua. I think we need to call in some reinforcements."

"Who are you thinking? Edward and Trevor? Trevor is a detective." Mathilde reaches for her phone, but I lay a hand on her arm to stop her.

"Trevor is a detective in England. While he knows more about chasing clues than the rest of us combined, that would be his only advantage if he came here. It's not like he can walk into the local station and announce he's investigating a fifty-year-old arson case that was deemed an accident."

"Especially not if his only reason for getting involved is because a ghost told him it wasn't an accident," Kate adds. "Bartie is out as well. Until we can create the connection between Padua and the magical field, he won't be able to interact with anyone or anything here."

I slump against the back of the sofa, frustrated by our lack of options. Edward, Trevor, and Bartie would happily drop everything and come here if we asked, but what would be the point?

I can't help feeling like we're missing something, and sitting around isn't helping. No one is surprised when I get up and grab a notebook from my bag. With my trusty pen in hand, I can already feel my brain kicking into action.

We haven't had any luck starting with the people we know. What if we think about the help we need and then see if anyone fits the bill?

Mathilde watches as I write a list of criteria for our ideal helper, reminding me to read aloud for everyone else's benefit.

"We should begin with the people who knew Angelina best. I'm assuming that is your family, Lavinia. Will it upset them if we ask questions?"

"No, I don't think so. My nonna loves to talk about Angelina. She says it keeps her alive in her memories. Mama must also remember her. Maybe if we speak to them together?" she trails off as she considers the approach. "Harry, I don't want to put you on the spot, but introducing you to my family would certainly give us an excuse to talk to them. We could say you are interested in learning about your historical Italian twin."

"We won't even have to lie," Harry agrees. "Even if Angelina's death wasn't suspicious, I'd still be curious to know more about her."

I tick an item off my list. "The remaining items are where things get tricky. I've written that we should interview people outside of your family, ideally anyone still alive from Angelina's circle of friends. It would also be very useful to get our hands on a copy of the original police report on the fire. Even if the investigators declared it an accident, given someone died, I'm sure they must have investigated the case."

"And now we're back to needing someone like Trevor in our group..." Mathilde crosses her arms, deep in thought.

"Forse... maybe..." Lavinia starts and stops abruptly, but not before she attracts everyone's attention.

"If you've got an idea, please share it," Kate encourages her.

"We're all flying by the seat of our pants. You can't do any worse than the rest of us."

Lavinia bites her lip, her eyes shifting as she weighs whether it is worth continuing. Finally, she works up the courage to speak aloud.

"I know someone who works for the polizia. I could ask him for help, but it would require us telling someone else about the magic. It's the only way I can explain why we need his help."

No one says no, but neither does anyone jump in with a resounding yes. I tap my pen against my chin, searching for options. "Do we have to tell him everything? Couldn't we try using the Harry has a twin story first? Or say we're writing a book about it? Mathilde's a researcher... she could be our writer."

"I love a good book as much as anyone else, but I hardly think I could masquerade as a writer," Mathilde counters.

Lavinia is shaking her head as well. "Filippo knows me and my family too well to buy that lie. Our family is very private, and Nonna would never condone us turning Angelina's life into fodder for a story, especially one written by a foreigner. I'd have to be honest with him. He'll see straight through any excuse, no matter how good it is."

"Lavinia's right." I clear my throat when everyone looks my way. "Think back to when Edward was investigating the murder at Barnard. We spent as much time hiding the magic from him as we did looking for clues. If Lavinia's friend is any good at his job, he'll sniff out the lie before we solve the case."

Harry speaks up from her seat on the other side of the room. "Perhaps you could tell us more about this Filippo, Lavinia. How do you know him?"

"Filippo is my brother-in-law. On my husband's side of the family," she quickly clarifies. "He is married to Stefano's sister. While we aren't related by blood, I have known him since we were little."

"Would you trust him with your life?" Harry asks.

"I've trusted him with my children's lives, on many an occasion. I get your point, though. This is an incredible secret. I know Filippo will respect the need to limit who knows magic exists. He won't stand by and let a murderer get away with it, even if the investigation is unorthodox."

"That's good enough for me." Harry checks to see if anyone feels differently. Kate, Mathilde, and I share similar solemn looks as we add our voices to the matter.

But there is still one vote left.

"H, what do you think? Would you be okay with Lavinia telling her brother-in-law about the Eternals? We'll need your help to convince him what she says is the truth. If you have any reservations, tell us now."

H flaps his wings, leaping from the window onto the arm of the sofa. His yellow eyes glow when he answers my question. "Someone attacked us tonight. There was only so much I could do to keep us safe. Iffen it's a matter of protecting 'Arry and you other missies, I'll take all the 'elp I can get."

Lavinia sighs in relief, happy to have found a solution. But her smile quickly flattens when it hits her what she has to do next.

"I think it's best if I first speak with him on my own. However, I'd appreciate your help with framing the conversation."

We spend the next half hour brainstorming ways to tell someone magic exists. The conversation starts off well, with me taking copious notes, but soon enough takes a turn for the absurd. By the time Lavinia decides she has enough to make a start of it, we're wiping tears of laughter from our cheeks.

"We needed that laugh," Kate admits as she stares at the line of mascara on her hand. "So we're agreed. You'll call Filippo tomorrow morning and ask him to meet you for a coffee. We'll stay close by, ready to come over as soon as you are ready for us to join in."

Lavinia gathers her coat and scarf, preparing to take her leave. We make her promise to take a taxi instead of walking across town on her own in the dark. Although it's barely ten in the evening, after our experience in the graveyard, none of us fancies a stroll through the shadows.

I tug my wyvern's spiky tail, pulling his attention away from the window. "H, why don't you keep Lavinia company while she walks to the nearest taxi stand?"

"Will do, Nat. Iffen anyone comes near, I'll blast 'em with my flames." He punctuates his statement with a tendril of black smoke.

Before the pair leave, Mathilde asks one last question. "Lavinia, how do you think Filippo will react to the news? Does he have any interest in the fantastical?"

"Filippo?" Lavinia shakes her head slowly, looking chagrinned. "He's much more of a *what you see is what you get* type of person. But he can hardly deny the truth when it stares him in the face."

"I know exactly the kind of man you mean," Mathilde agrees. "Trevor, my partner, is the same way. Coming face-to-face with a wyvern nearly scared him half to death, but it was surprisingly effective as a means of overcoming any doubts. Don't stress too much!"

"I'm not sure I can stop the stress entirely, but your words comfort me, Mathilde." Lavinia makes a last round of the group, air-kissing our cheeks in the standard Italian goodbye.

None of us relax until H returns to let us know Lavinia made it safely to her taxi. H sends us off to bed, saying he intends to keep watch for a while longer. I make sure he has a blanket on the sofa where he can curl up when he finally calls it a night.

In my bed, I toss and turn, unable to switch off my mind and get some rest. I refuse to consider what might happen if we fail to identify the evil spectre haunting Harry. Lavinia's brother-in-law has to help us. One way or another, we'll do whatever it takes to identify Angelina's killer and see justice served.

❖

The night passes peacefully, and the next morning, I find H snoozing in a puddle of sunshine. When Kate steps out of her room, I hold my finger to my mouth, asking her to keep quiet. Our brave winged companion deserves his rest after keeping us all safe.

After dashing off a quick note to let H know where we've gone, the four of us pop out for cappuccinos and croissants at the nearby bakery. Over breakfast, I wait for someone to bring up the events of the day before. I'm certain that one of my friends must have second thoughts at this point. It would be completely natural after the experience.

However, a night of rest seems to have only strengthened everyone's resolve. We eat our breakfast in relative silence. We're all too caught up in our thoughts of the day ahead to waste our time forcing a conversation.

With a takeaway bag in hand, we return to our rental flat and find H waking up. He grumbles about being left behind until I produce the paper bag with the cream-filled brioche inside. The flaky pastry leaves him covered with crumbs, but a quick jet of flames does the trick of tidying his scales better than any wet cloth.

"Any word from Lavinia?" I ask. Kate pulls her phone from her pocket and scowls at the blank screen.

The four walls of the flat seem far too small. By mutual agreement, we decide to head out. There are still plenty of things we could visit but none of us has any interest in sightseeing today.

The cobblestone streets are slick with dew. Humidity thickens the air and I can already tell the day will be a warm one. We stick to the covered walkways, meandering along the pavement as we check out the window displays. Despite the colourful fabrics and eye-catching designs, I can hardly work up the interest to do more than glance as we go along. On any other day, I'd been over the moon at getting a day to shop in Italy. This morning, however, clothes are the furthest thing from my mind.

We're all on edge, jumping anytime we hear a mobile phone ring. H weaves in and out of the legs of the other pedestrians in his effort to keep watch over us. I keep my focus on Harry. Every time she stops, I'm right there with her. With a crazed ghost on the loose, I don't dare leave her open to any other surprises.

When Kate's phone finally buzzes with an incoming message, we all breathe a sigh of relief.

"Lavinia asks us to come straight away."

"Fine with me," I agree, already turning in the right direction. We're only minutes away from her house, having wandered ever closer as the morning went on. Kate presses the buzzer on the front gate and waves at the camera when Lavinia's voice comes over the speaker. When the gate opens, we hurry up the path to her house.

I can feel sweat beading on my forehead. I'm not sure whether it is due to the rising temperatures or my nerves. In all likelihood, it is the combination which is doing me in. If Filippo agrees to help us, I'm confident we can identify Angelina's murderer before it is time for us to return to Oxford.

Lavinia opens the front door before we can knock, stepping into the gap to keep us from coming inside. I expect to see a welcoming smile. Instead, her brow is furrowed and her lips are flat against her teeth.

"We've got a problem."

My heart stutters as my mind races through the possibilities.

"Filippo refuses to believe me. He thinks I'm playing a joke on him."

Although Lavinia's voice is thick with worry, I'm almost relieved that this is our issue. "It's okay," I reassure her. I point over my shoulder to where H is hovering at the back of our group. "I've been through this before. As soon as he sees our wyvern's true identity, he'll have to believe."

"I hope so. Come on in. He's sitting in the kitchen."

We troop through the house and enter the kitchen. A man sits at the breakfast table with his back to us. In my head, I'd been picturing an officer in a uniform, but Filippo is wearing a crisp, white, buttoned shirt. He shifts slowly in his chair, angling until he can see our faces.

He gives each of us a wide smile, putting my worries at ease as he stands up to shake our hands. We take turns introducing ourselves. I start, giving him my name and H's as well. Mathilde and Kate are right behind me. Harry comes up last.

Filippo's eyes widen when she steps in front of him. "Wow, Lavinia! You weren't kidding. She is the spitting image of your zia."

Lavinia raps Filippo on the arm. "I told you I wasn't making this up. Now sit down, and listen to us."

Filippo and Lavinia might not be related, but their body language and rapport are so much like a brother and sister that I have to stifle a laugh. We take seats around Lavinia's kitchen table, giving me the chance to get a better look at Filippo.

His light brown hair is on the longish side, brushing the back of his shirt collar. His hazel eyes twinkle with some unspoken joke. He introduces himself, waving his hands around as he talks. Filippo is every inch the easy-going Italian.

He gives me a mock-stern look, motioning to where H sits in my lap. "Lavinia expects me to believe your cat can talk. I suppose you have some video you want me to watch where he yowls a word-like sound. Or is he capable of performing on command?"

"Yowl-like sound?" H fumes. "I'll show 'im a performance 'e'll never forget."

Mathilde snickers at H's outrage, while Filippo's laugh rolls across the table.

"I see what you mean, Lavinia. It does almost seem like the cat is responding to what I'm saying." Filippo reaches across the table to pat H on the head, but jerks his hand back when H shows his fangs. "Not very friendly, though."

Lavinia rolls her eyes at her friend. "I told you, Filippo. H isn't a cat, he's a wyvern, There's a whole world of magic hidden from our view, where ghosts walk among us and fantastical creatures exist."

Filippo waits a beat for Lavinia to admit the joke. When she stares at him, refusing to back down, his brow wrinkles in confusion. "Are you listening to yourself? You want me to believe in magic? We're not children any longer."

"I know it is hard to believe, but I'm telling you the truth. I'm not coming to you because you are my friend, but because you're an officer with the polizia. A terrible crime happened in the past, and if we don't solve it, we risk seeing someone else get hurt. Stop joking around and pay attention, Filippo."

Filippo's expression changes, the humour draining from his face as he leans forward, resting his hands on the table. "What do you want me to do, Lavinia? File a report saying a ghost is attacking people? At best, I'd be laughed out of the station. Worst case, you'd be fined for filing a false report." He scans our faces and adds, "All of you would be fined. It is better for everyone if you drop the prank now. We can enjoy an espresso and then I'll go back to work. No harm done."

"No harm done?" Harry echoes. "My life is at risk. I know you don't know me from Adam, but we are exactly who we proclaim to be — representatives from the University of Oxford here for the twin city project. We came here with the best of intentions and stumbled into a scenario even we couldn't have imagined. We have no choice but to investigate Angelina's death and stop whatever maddened spirit is haunting me, simply because I look like Angelina. Lavinia thinks you can help us. If you won't do it for me, do it for her."

"Please, Filippo," Lavinia says. "I was skeptical at first, just like you. But once they brought me into their circle and gave me the ability to see the magical spirits around us, I couldn't deny the truth. If you will hold hands with the cat, you'll see for yourself."

Filippo jerks his head back. "I'm not holding hands with a cat, Lavinia. Especially not one who growled at me a few moments ago. If you say there is a crime, where is the proof? I need something I can hang an investigation upon — something which doesn't require so-called cat magic to see."

H's nostrils send swirls of smoke into my face. I feel the same frustration with how the conversation is going. We can't force Filippo to join hands with us so he can gain the ability to see the real H. But maybe we don't need to convince him of the magical aspects.

"Will it help if I tell you who discovered the magical field? It was a group of scientists, or natural philosophers, as they were called. Sir Christopher Wren stumbled across the existence while at Oxford. Even Sir Isaac Newton knew magic was real. If they can believe it, why can't you?"

Filippo crosses his arms over his chest. His posture tells me there's no point in continuing to focus on the past. He won't listen unless he can see something with his own eyes.

"If you want proof — modern day proof — I'll give you two examples. The first is that Harry took a very public spill down the stairs at the Santo yesterday. The priest on duty will surely remember as he rushed over to check on us."

"The second is Mrs Bakker," Harry adds. "She was nearly killed yesterday when our ghost pushed her over the balcony at the Anatomical Theatre. She gave a statement to the guards. You can follow up with her and see for yourself how similar she looks to me. Same build, same hair colour. From the back, it would be easy to make a mistake."

"That's the truth," Mathilde whispers to me. I shiver as I recall the moment I thought it was Harry lying dead.

"Whether you want to believe, I'm convinced the current problems are somehow connected to Angelina." Lavinia crosses her arms, her expression grim. "We're going to investigate her death, Filippo. If you truly value our friendship, you will help us."

"Santo cielo, Lavinia!" he moans. "Of course, I value our friendship. You are my family! But this is my job. I can't go waving my badge around to force people to talk about an accident that happened fifty years ago. How would I explain any of this to my superiors?"

Tension builds in the room as Filippo and Lavinia stare at one another, deadlocked in their positions. I'd suggest we walk away from the idea of getting his help, but when I see Harry sitting there, I know I'll do whatever it takes to keep her safe. In this case, it means finding a middle ground.

I clear my throat to get Filippo's attention. "It's true. We need the detection skills you've honed in your job, but I don't think a badge is necessarily a requirement. You and Lavinia are friends. What if you helped her informally? We're not asking you to arrest anyone. You couldn't even if you wanted to do so!"

Filippo leans back in his chair and sighs, knowing we've backed him into a corner. All around me, my friends are giving him the same beseeching look. "Va bene, Lavinia. I will do what I can, but only that which is within reason. First, however, I intend to verify the information you gave me about the incident at the Santo and Mrs Bakker."

"Grazie, Filippo! I knew I could count on you." Lavinia leans over and gives her friend a hug and then steps away from the table. "Get out that notebook of yours and take down the information. I will make everyone an espresso. We will need our energy for what comes next."

Chapter Ten

After Filippo leaves for his office at the police station, I offer to lend a hand with washing up the cups before we make our departure.

Lavinia waves off my offer and tells us to keep our seats. "I hope you don't mind, but I've arranged for us to speak with my mother and nonna today. When I told Nonna how much Harry resembles Angelina, she insisted we come for lunch."

"That's very generous of her, but we don't want to make your grandmother go to so much trouble," Kate replies. "Can we bring something over?"

"We can pick up some dolcetti on the way. As for the rest, don't worry. Nonna loves cooking for people. It makes her feel useful when she can do something for others."

We don't have long to wait before it is time to leave. Lavinia tells us more about her neighbourhood as we detour to the pastry shop on our way to her grandmother's house. She mixes stories from her childhood together with historical facts, painting a picture of Padua only a local would know.

All too soon, she unlocks a gate and leads us along a drive of crushed shells toward a home. "I grew up in this house," she explains. "As did my mother and my grandmother. It's been in our family for a century."

The house is three-stories tall, with large windows framed with wooden shutters. Painted in terracotta orange tones, it sits against a backdrop of old evergreen trees and thick grass.

The front door opens, and a wizened old woman bids us to hurry inside. She squeezes Kate's hands, saying she remembers her from Lavinia's wedding. Harry is next in line. When Lavinia's grandmother sees her, she swoons and her eyes fill with tears.

I bite my lip, worrying this was a mistake. Perhaps seeing her sister's face on someone else will be too much for the old woman.

But no, Nonna is stronger than that. She pulls Harry close, not asking for permission as she places her hands on either side of Harry's face. Her scrutiny is intense as she studies Harry's face from every angle.

"So much like our Angelina," she murmurs. "But the nose is different... the eyebrows thicker." Nonna steps back and drops her hands. She smiles at Harry. "Angelina would have given her right arm for eyebrows like yours. She was forever shading them with her eye pencil."

Another woman bustles into the entry from deeper within the house, immediately identifiable as Lavinia's mother. The family resemblance is strong across the three generations.

"Mamma, let the women get inside," she chastises, inviting us into the front room. Around we go again with telling our names and what we do. Lavinia's mum is also struck by how much Harry looks like her late zia, but thankfully doesn't have as strong an emotional reaction. As soon as we're past the intros, her nonna invites us to the dining room.

The furniture is as old as the house, but marred with the tiny imperfections that come from years of use. Dozens of paintings, large and small, decorate the walls, illuminated by a Venetian glass chandelier. The table is set with a linen tablecloth, white plates, and crystal glasses.

"You shouldn't have gone to so much trouble," Harry gasps when she sees the setting.

"This is how Nonna always prepares the table," Lavinia assures her. "Dio save us if we forget to put out the tablecloth!"

"My mother brought me up to prepare a proper table," Nonna replies, unbothered by her granddaughter's teasing. "You were, too, although you like to pretend otherwise."

"And on that note," Lavinia's mum intervenes, "why don't you help me bring in the food, Lavinia?"

Over a lunch of pumpkin risotto and homemade bread, we learn more about Angelina from the women who knew her well.

"Angelina was my older sister," Nonna begins. "She was ten when I was born, and for the first few years of my life, she was convinced I was her toy and not a person. By the time I was walking and talking enough to be a proper playmate, she was a moody teenager."

"When did you two become close?" Lavinia asks.

"Not until after the death of her husband. I must have been around fourteen or fifteen when it happened. Old enough to understand that she was heartbroken, but too young to know how to help her deal with the loss. Our loss, I should say. I loved him as much as she did. He was as gorgeous as any movie star. When he came around, I could barely string two words together." Nonna laughs, lost in her memory. "He only had eyes for Angelina. Thought he was invincible, and that was what killed him in the end. He injured himself working in the garden and refused to see a doctor. The wound turned septic, and he was gone."

We studiously avoid looking at Nonna as she dabs a tear from her eye.

"Angelina was practically catatonic after it happened. Our mamma told me to give her space, so I did. Her best friend Rosa rushed over to take care of her and to coax her back into the real world once the initial grief passed. Angelina never remarried, though. She said it wouldn't be right."

My friends and I are dumbstruck by this unexpected story of love and loss. It's all I can do to avoid imagining myself in the same circumstance. What if something happened to Edward? My heart squeezes at the merest notion and I have to stifle that thought before it can take root.

Having heard the story before, Lavinia is the first to recover. "But Zia Angelina dated men. I've seen photos of her at events and parties. There was always a man on her arm or standing nearby."

Nonna grins. "There was no shortage of men who fancied Angelina. Our mamma was desperate for nipoti — grandbabies, you call them. Every time Angelina would start seeing a new man, Mamma would be convinced that this was the one who would coax Angelina into taking a second chance at a family. Angelina knew what Mamma desired, but she wasn't about to be pressured into doing anything she didn't want. She'd date the men just long enough for Mamma to get her hopes up, and then she'd break things off and move on to the next."

"Our Angelina was very avante garde," Lavinia's mum adds. "This was a long time ago, when society looked much less favourably on women. She was a widow, and that status granted her a certain amount of freedom. It was like she'd decided that if she couldn't have the life she wanted, she'd make the most of what was left for her. No husband and no children, but she found other ways to have fun."

"My kind of woman," Kate pipes up. Since Kate is forty and dating an Eternal, with no plans to have children, she is the closest person in our group to Angelina. I can imagine Kate making a similar decision, attending all the best events with whatever man struck her fancy.

Lavinia's mum gives Kate a warm smile, acknowledging their similarities. "I idolised Angelina. Whenever I went to her house, she'd let me dress up in her fancy clothes and jewellery. Even though she never remarried, she still taught me a lot about relationships and what to look for in a partner." She gives Lavinia a wink. "Thanks to her, I know exactly how to keep your papa in his place."

Lavinia bursts into a laugh at her mother's quip. "And you passed all that knowledge down a generation. Based on how well my girls manage Stefano, I think we can safely assume they're also paying attention. Their poor future husbands don't have a chance."

Their affection for one another is contagious and has all of us grinning around the dining table. Watching their banter makes me think of my mum and dad. Despite living in different countries and speaking another language, the meaning of family transcends the borders. It doesn't take any effort to imagine me and my mum having a similar conversation in the future. I make a mental note to call her later, just to say hello.

"There was one man who stuck around much longer than any other." Nonna says. "His name was Marco. He was a little older than Angelina, and very active on the social scene. They found themselves at the same events so often that they joked they might as well show up together."

"Marco was never Angelina's fidanzato, mamma," Lavinia's mum corrects. "They were best friends, but that was the limit of their relationship."

"You don't know that for sure," Nonna replies, sitting up straighter. "You were so young. Angelina would not confide in you about her love life."

I expect Lavinia's mum to back down, but to my surprise, she shakes off her mother's remark and retorts with one of her own.

"I know more than you think, Mamma! I kept a secret for Zia

Angelina for all these years." She takes a deep breath and decides to share. "I suppose since she is no longer with us, there's no harm in telling you now."

"You hid something from me!" Nonna gasps, her face growing red. "About my sister!"

"I honoured her wishes. I'm sure she had her reasons for wanting to keep this relationship a secret. But, as you said, I was too young for her to share what they were. And before you get angry, I should say that I only know because I saw them with my own eyes."

Nonna's flash of anger burns out as fast as it appeared. "Saw whom? Angelina and someone else?"

Lavinia's mum nods her head. "Shortly before her death, I showed up at Angelina's house unexpectedly. I burst in the door without knocking and found Angelina and a man embracing on her sofa. Angelina swore me to secrecy. I'd never seen her so upset. I complied without a second of hesitation. After she died, it felt like an even bigger betrayal to tell you anything about it. So I kept it to myself. Until now, that is."

Nonna gives her daughter a wobbly smile. "I understand now. I'm still mad you didn't eventually tell me, but at least you had a good reason."

Lavinia and the rest of us are on the edges of our seats. Finally, a piece of information which might give us a lead for our investigation into Angelina's death.

"Who was it, Mamma?" Lavinia asks. "The man that you saw. Did you know him?"

"His name is Paolo Pavan."

"Our commercialista?" Nonna exclaims. "I sat across from him at meetings for years. He never mentioned anything about Angelina. Never gave me even a hint that there was something between them."

I glance at Lavinia to see if she knows the man. She takes the hint and poses a question.

"You said his name is... does that mean he's still alive?"

"Si, Lavinia. He is closer to my age. I know we're old, but we're not ready for the graveyard just yet."

Lavinia's mum rolls her eyes. "You've got more energy than I do, Mamma. Like cheese and wine, you seem to get bolder with age."

The conversation turns to other topics as we linger over dessert and espresso. Lavinia's mum and grandmother regale us with stories of their childhoods in Padua. Listening to them is like sitting with an Eternal in Oxford. There is no match for hearing firsthand experiences in order to understand the history of a city.

Although we came to lunch with the intention of learning about Angelina, I walk away with fresh ideas of how we might honour the new connection between Oxford and Padua. That's a good thing given Harry and I are expected to sit in planning meetings in the coming days.

Before we leave, Harry asks Nonna if she has any other photos of Angelina's, or any of her old things.

"Sí, cara," she answers, patting Harry's hand. "The boxes and trunks are in the attic. I couldn't bear to part with them, but I haven't been up there in years."

"Would you mind if we have a look?" Mathilde asks. When Nonna arches an eyebrow at the unorthodox request, Mathilde explains, "I'm a historian. For me, it would be like finding a time capsule. I'd love to see her old clothes, books, photos... anything!"

Nonna thinks for a moment before giving her approval. "I'm sure you will know how to handle her things with care. I will say yes, with one condition."

"What's that?" Mathilde replies.

"That you will agree to bring me down some photos and her diaries. I'm too old to climb up there, but I'd love to see her gorgeous, smiling face again. The items you bring me will fill in the gaps that the years have made in my memories."

"It's a deal," Mathilde pledges. "We'll do everything we can to give you the chance to see Angelina again, exactly as you remember her."

❖

It's late in the afternoon when Lavinia calls with news from Filippo. Kate answers and puts it on speakerphone so we can all hear.

"Filippo's asked to meet us. I've suggested your flat, since it is the quietest location available. I hope that's okay."

"Of course, it's fine. What time should we expect you?"

"We'll be there in an hour. He said he doesn't have long, so no need to think about organising dinner."

"It's a plan. We'll see you soon," Kate confirms.

"Am I the only one who feels nervous?" I scan Kate's face for any signs of her thoughts.

"No, Nat. It seems ridiculous to be so tense. After all, Filippo is Lavinia's close friend. He said he'd help as long as our story checks out. It would only take him a couple of phone calls to verify everything."

"And yet..." my voice trails off. I go quiet as I try to put my finger on what is bothering me.

Surprisingly, it's H who comes through with the answer.

"It's the magical 'elp you're missing, Nat. Iffen we were in Oxford, we Eternals would whisper in the right ear and open doors wherever you needed to go."

Mathilde freezes in place, as taken aback as I am. The look on her face makes me laugh at the both of us. "A year ago, I didn't know magic existed. Now I depend upon it. It's incredible how much your life can change."

Harry, ever the voice of reason, joins the conversation. "I'm not so sure that there isn't some kind of magic at work here. What are the odds that I'd visit Padua with the only people in the world who'd have a chance at solving this mystery?"

"She's right," Kate adds. She pauses her task of carrying more chairs into our sitting room. "I'm more convinced than ever that Padua is meant to be the next connection point to the magical field."

I ponder her words as we get everything set up for Filippo and Lavinia's arrival. We're very lucky to have Lavinia as our first prefect. However, it wouldn't be fair to leave her on her own with such an enormous responsibility. Sir Christopher Wren had the help of his Philosophical Club when he discovered how to connect Oxford to the magical field. Four centuries later, it still takes three of us to keep the magical connection in place. We each have our own sphere of responsibility — and doing our part is a full-time job.

Lavinia is perfectly suited to be the new Kate, but who will oversee the books like Mathilde, or the people and ceremonies like I do?

I'm no closer to an answer when the doorbell rings, announcing our visitors' arrival.

Lavinia enters first, trailing her floral perfume through our rental flat as she makes the rounds. Even though it's only been a few hours since we last saw her, she still takes the time to buss light kisses on all our cheeks. Filippo follows behind her, limiting himself to a handshake.

I know I shouldn't read anything into his body language, but I can't stop myself from wondering whether there's a reason he's keeping us at arms-length.

We take seats in the small sitting room. Mathilde and I choose the sofa, with H perching on the arm at my side. Kate and Harry move to the wooden dining table chairs, leaving the more comfortable armchairs for Filippo and Lavinia. If Lavinia knows what Filippo has to say, she doesn't reveal it in her expression.

When we're all settled, Filippo leans forward, resting his elbows on his knees. He gazes around the room, meeting each of our eyes. I'm on the edge of my seat by the time he speaks.

"I have known Lavinia for most of my life. She is more than a friend... she is part of my family. While I trust her to be honest with me, I also wouldn't put it past her to play a joke. This is why I had to verify what you told me."

None of us move.

"I worked through the events in the order you said they happened. I called the diocese and got through to the priest who was on duty on the day you said you tumbled. I had limited hopes he would remember a small incident, especially given the number of people who pass through the Santo every day. But he remembered you. He recalled the entire group and became immediately worried because an officer was phoning. I spent more time reassuring him you were fine than I did getting the story from him."

"The case of Mrs Bakker was even easier to review. My colleague was already investigating the incident — a serious one, by any standards. For a tourist to be attacked in my city, that is not something we'd let pass unchecked. My colleague had commandeered the available security footage from the area. I watched it myself, checking the timestamps to see when your group entered and exited the space."

Harry interrupts, saying, "You thought we might have been responsible, didn't you? If Lavinia wasn't playing a prank on you, you had to consider we might be up to no good."

Filippo nods. "I searched your names and photos, making sure you are who you claim to be. I cannot deny that something is afoot, but a supernatural explanation?" He scoffs in disdain. "I'm not ready to make that leap."

"Filippo!" Lavinia gasps. Filippo holds up a hand to stop her before she can chastise him.

"I'm not saying I won't help you. You claim Harry's tumble and the attack on Mrs Bakker are related. If there is any chance that is true, it is my responsibility as a poliziotto to look into the matter. I can hardly pass your information to a colleague, not so long as you are babbling about supernatural explanations. It would reflect poorly on both me and Lavinia."

"We're not babbling," Lavinia corrects him. Her face is flushed in anger at his dismissal of our claims.

"I don't want to argue with you, Lavinia," he answers in a soothing tone. "But I am a man of the facts. In my years on the police force, I've never encountered a crime that wasn't committed by man. My colleagues will work on the traditional channels of investigation. There is no harm in me accompanying you while you search for a connection behind a past accident and what is happening now. Worst case, I waste my time. Better case, I find a logical explanation for these potentially unconnected events."

"You forgot the best case," Kate chimes in. "You find we're telling the truth and right a wrong that has stood for half a century."

Filippo gives a small shake of his head, amused at our insistence that there is more to the world than what the eye can see. As much as it galls me to have to depend upon someone who thinks we are liars or fools, deep inside, I know Filippo is our best option. It's more important to identify the ghostly Eternal who is causing so much trouble than it is to have Filippo admit we might be right.

I grab my notebook from the coffee table and flip to the page where I'd already started organising my thoughts.

"I'll make note of your position on the matter, Filippo. We appreciate your help, especially given you are making what must feel like a leap of faith. I can only give you my word that we are on the right track. Until we identify the culprit, there's no point in arguing over the matter. Now, let's move on to the tactical side of the plan."

Filippo raises an eyebrow. "You have some suggestions?"

"You have no idea..." Mathilde mumbles, only loud enough for me to hear. She knows all too well how much I love making a list.

I ignore her comment and focus on the task at hand. "We only have five days left in Padua, so we need to be efficient. I've separated our avenues for investigation into three groups. The first is to look through Angelina's old things in storage at Nonna's house. Since Mathilde already got permission to go through them, I suggest she and Harry work together."

I glance at the two to see if they agree. Harry gives me a thumbs up, but Mathilde is biting her lip. "What's the matter?"

"Err, one small problem. Harry and I don't speak Italian. We can look through the photos, but how will we read any notes we find?"

"Hmm," I murmur. I hadn't considered that angle.

H comes again to the rescue. "I can go wiff 'em," he offers. "There's nothing we Eternals can't understand."

"Excellent." I jot a quick note on my pad. "Mathilde, Harry, and H will search the attic."

Out of the corner of my eye, I spy on Filippo's reaction to the discussion. While we heard H speaking in plain English, all Filippo heard was a miaow. I have to bite my lip to keep from laughing when I see his mouth hanging open. He closes it, and reopens it as though preparing to speak. But his logical brain kicks in before he can form the question of why adding a cat to the team solves the language barrier.

I smoothly move onto my next point. "Thinking about Angelina's personal items made me recognise there is another tranche of materials available. A fire where someone lost their life

— an event like that would have been covered in the news and had at least a cursory investigation. Lavinia and Kate, would you two be up for some searches through the local library archives? And Filippo, could you get copies of the police file?"

"I can do that," he agrees. "Since it is a closed case and an old one, at that, there shouldn't be an issue with me pulling the records from our system. I'll print the materials and bring them over tomorrow. However, I assumed that was what you wanted me to do. If I'm not going through the police files, what's my role?"

"We need you to do what you do best," I reply. "Our conversation with Lavinia's mum and grandmother shed light on at least one potential suspect. A secret love interest. I suggest we pay him a visit."

"We?" Filippo raises both eyebrows. "Do you mean to come along?"

"Yes, for two reasons. The first is because, within the group, I have the most relevant experience of questioning suspects. In Oxford, I've established a good working relationship with a detective on the police force. The second is because we need someone there who is at least willing to consider that the real culprit is dead. While you can look for living people who might hold a grudge, I can dig for insights on those who are dead."

Filippo is so taken aback that for a moment, I half expect him to retract his agreement to work alongside us. But one look at Lavinia's face and he straightens up, wiping the incredulous expression from his face. His mouth flattens into a straight line as he bites back any argument.

"Va bene," he agrees, his tone making it clear he is doing so out of obligation. "Who is this person we need to meet?"

Lavinia answers. "His name is Paolo Pavan. He's expecting you to come to his home tomorrow morning."

"You booked a meeting before I agreed to help?" Filippo asks.

"Caro Filippo, I told Paolo that a lovely young woman from Oxford wanted to speak with him. He is an old man and is happy to have any visitors. Your presence there will be an unexpected bonus."

We wrap up our meeting in short order by agreeing to meeting times and locations. Tomorrow is our last full day before Harry and I are expected to attend meetings with the twinning ceremony planning committee. We need to make the most of it.

We see Lavinia and Filippo out the door, making sure to thank them both for their help. Kate shuts the door behind them and turns to face the rest of us.

"Anyone want to place a bet on how long it takes Filippo to admit we're telling the truth, and that magic is real?"

Laughter booms as every single one of us nods our agreement.

"Where are you going?" Kate calls when I spin around and head for the sitting room.

"Where else?" I reply, brandishing my notepad. "Someone needs to write the bets, and I can't see any of you doing it. Who wants to go first?"

I laugh even harder as my friends throw out their best guesses, treasuring this rare moment of levity in the midst of a very stressful situation.

Chapter Eleven

Filippo texts me to meet him outside the next morning. My ladybird dress had seemed perfectly appropriate when I'd gotten ready in the warm flat. Now, in the chilly morning air, I'm second-guessing that choice. A cool breeze sends my skirt twirling around my legs, giving me goose pimples. A jaunty red Fiat pulls up at the kerb and I sigh in relief when I see Filippo behind the wheel.

"Buon giorno," he announces as I close the door and buckle my seatbelt. He swings onto the road with hardly a glance around him, miraculously avoiding a scooter and two pedestrians as he drives out of the centre. He shifts from one gear to another, acting more like a Formula One driver than a responsible officer of the law.

He knows the area better than the back of his hand, zipping up narrow one-way streets and speeding past the long stone walls that surround the historic centre. I catch myself bracing for impact, thrown as much by being on the wrong side of the road as by the passing scenery. Filippo catches sight of my death grip on my seatbelt and suggests getting to know one another might prove a better distraction than watching the world pass outside the windshield.

"Signor Pavan retired to the countryside years ago. We've got a half-hour drive in front of us. Why don't you tell me how you ended up working at Oxford?"

"That's a short story," I begin, already smiling as I think about the man who inspired me. "My father grew up in Oxford. My grandfather worked for one of the college libraries. When I was little, he told me mesmerising stories about a magical world. Little did I know he was telling the truth. Fate ensured I was in the right place at the right time, and applied for the Head of Ceremonies role when it came open."

Filippo gives me a bland look at my casual use of the word magical, but refuses to take the bait. I debate pushing the envelope but ultimately decide that it isn't worth forcing it. I have to believe that he'll come around eventually or else it doesn't matter. He's here helping, and that's what counts.

Instead, I tell him a little about Edward and the surprise discovery that I'd inherited a house. For his part, Filippo asks me about Oxford and how it compares to what I've seen of Padua so far. After a while, I turn the discussion his way.

"What about you, Filippo? I know you're married to Lavinia's sister-in-law, and that you must have grown up in Padua to have known Lavinia for so long. But surely there's more to your life story."

"That about covers it. I've been here since the day I was born, just like the other members of my family. I could never imagine moving around like you've done."

"So you always dreamt of becoming a police officer?"

"No," he admits, chuckling. "I thought I'd be a historian at one point in my life. Then, I got called to do my military service and found the rank and order to be very comforting. I knew where I fit, if that makes sense. When my year was up, I came back to Padova and applied to join the police force. Twenty years later, I'm still here."

"What about your love of history? Did you abandon that dream?"

"Not all together." Filippo reaches into the back seat to grab something. After a second, he straightens up and hands me a hardback. "This is the textbook for the class I'm taking right now."

I glance at the title, stumbling in my attempt to translate the Italian title into something I can understand. Filippo laughs at my horrid pronunciation and finally puts me out of my misery.

"It's a class on the history of the Medici Court and its impact. I picked it because I wanted to learn more about Galileo. Did you know he made his discovery that the Earth orbits the sun right here in Padova?" When I nod, his smile grows even wider. "I take one class each term, just for fun."

"That's not a bad idea," I agree. "At the rate my life is going, I should take some criminal justice classes at Oxford. Although, maybe not ones taught by my fiancé."

"Because you'd be afraid he'd play favourites?"

"Oh no, not Edward. It would be the reverse. He'd be twice as hard on me, and would do something evil like surprising me with a pop quiz at the breakfast table." The thought of Edward grilling me over a bowl of cereal reminds me of why I'm in the car with Filippo, driving through the Italian countryside. As delightful as the conversation has been so far, it's time I got it back on course.

"We should probably talk about what to say to Signor Pavan before we get there. Did Lavinia share with you what her mum told us?"

"I saw Lavinia this morning when I dropped off the copies of the case file. However, she didn't have time to tell me anything, as I was running late. I assumed you'd be able to update me."

"No problem. I came prepared." I'm not exaggerating. The

notebook and pen are tucked in my handbag. "Before I go through my notes, did the old case files shed any light on the cause of the fire?"

"I flipped through them while they printed. From what I could see, they put the cause down to a gas leak. Most houses have gas for cooking, and it isn't outside of the realm of possibility that a leak could have resulted in an explosion. If Angelina forgot to turn off the cooktop knob, or had a frayed hose... it could have very easily been an accident."

My lips curl at this piece of unhelpful news. "I'd been hoping that there would be something there — some piece of evidence that techniques at the time couldn't analyse the way we can now. But a gas leak? That's not particularly unusual."

"Do you still want to stick to your story that something more is in play? If you want to back down from your statement that Angelina's case is connected to Mrs Bakker and Harry, now's your chance."

I give Filippo a hard look. "We're on the right track. If you'd open your mind to the existence of things you can't see, you'd understand why." I swallow my frustration, not wanting to argue. "What if we set aside what we know, and looked at some hypothetical scenarios? Given the cause of the fire, what might have made the fire investigators dig deeper?"

Filippo doesn't answer right away. I can see he's thinking through the question as he overtakes a slow-moving car.

"Maybe if Angelina's family had made a fuss at the time, or flagged some concern to the investigative team, perhaps they would have taken longer before declaring it an accident."

I can work with that answer. "All right, let's do that now. Lavinia is related to Angelina, and she's saying she doesn't buy the story that it was an accident. You're the investigator on the case. What do you do next?"

I catch Filippo's eye as he gives me a sideways glance, making note of the hint of admiration. As much as he doesn't want to play along, now that I've framed it properly, he feels compelled to answer me.

"Let me think. A gas leak must have happened inside the house. I can't imagine a random burglar choosing such an unpredictable method for covering their tracks. If you exclude a break-in, that would insinuate that it was either Angelina or someone she knew well enough to let into her house."

I glance at the bulleted list I created the night before, happy to see Filippo's train of thought is going in the same direction as my own.

Filippo is still talking his way through his answer. "I'd divide the people she knows into four groups, and work my way through them. Family first — although in this case, I'm willing to accept that they weren't involved. That leaves any romantic relationships, close friends, and known enemies."

That last item hadn't made my list. "Why known enemies? You said it had to be someone she'd let into her house. Do people normally invite their enemies in for a cup of espresso?"

Filippo snorts at my question. "You'd be amazed at some things I've seen during my years as a poliziotto, Nat. Sometimes people hope their enemy finally wants to make amends. Other times, they can't pass up the opportunity to make their enemies squirm."

"I know the old saying is to keep your friends close, but your enemies closer. However, I've met a few murderers in the past year and I've never had the inclination to invite them to my home."

Filippo is so shocked by my statement that he nearly runs off the road. "Why have you met murderers — plural — in the last year?"

I cock my head to the side and give him a sassy smile. "I could tell you, but you wouldn't believe me. Suffice it to say, I'm not a complete newbie when it comes to solving crimes. Which brings us back to Signor Pavan. According to Lavinia's mum, he and Angelina were engaged in a secret tryst. At the time, Angelina's usual escort was a man named Marco."

"Why aren't we going to see Marco?" Filippo asks. "He'd be at the top of my hypothetical list."

"Why else? He's dead. We are talking about a fifty-year-old case and the people involved weren't exactly spring chickens. We're lucky Signor Pavan is still alive."

Filippo turns my way, giving me a smirk. "I thought you could talk to ghosts. Isn't that what you claimed?"

"Not until we establish boundaries and connect Padua to what we call the magical field," I answer, shaking my head at his attempt to mark a smart remark. "You can't have it both ways, Filippo. If you want to know the ins and outs of how the magic works, you have to accept that it is real. Otherwise, let's stick to getting information from the people who are still breathing."

Filippo sighs heavily, looking skyward as if for help from a higher power. "The things I do for family," he mutters.

I studiously avoid looking at him, focusing on my notepad as I turn to the next page. "I've taken the liberty of drafting up a few questions for Signor Pavan. Shall I run through my list or do you have a standard set you prefer to use as a basis for getting started?"

Filippo lifts his hand from the wheel and waves it sideways, ceding the floor. "Let's hear your questions, Nat. But I should warn you. I've seen enough British crime shows to know how you work. Here in Italy, we take a very different approach to questioning suspects. Less inquisition, more casual chat. If we want the whole truth from Signor Pavan, we'll have to coax it out of him."

I shrug my shoulders at his remark, letting his words tumble down my back. From spending time with the Eternals, I know a fair bit about working across cultures. Brits today are a far cry from those who moved in society hundreds of years before. Plus, I know people. Figuring out how to put them at ease is my thing.

Nonetheless, I'm willing to watch and learn. If Filippo wants to kick off the conversation, who am I to stand in his way? But if he thinks we're leaving the Pavan house without getting the answers I seek, he's in for a rude awakening.

Filippo wasn't kidding when he said our destination was in the countryside. Fields of grapevines line the road as far as the eye can see. Somehow, Filippo spies the gap in the hedge that marks the drive and swings into it, hardly slowing down. He shifts the gears, bringing the car to a halt in front of a single-story home.

The house and setting are idyllic as the garden trellises gradually blend into the rows of vines. This late in the season, the vines are heavy with fruit. Harvest must be just around the corner. A compact car sits parked at the side of the rose-coloured house. In the middle of the garden is a wooden bench, perfectly positioned to catch the morning sun. It would be the ideal place to curl up with a book and a cuppa.

Unfortunately, I've got other tasks to accomplish, and basking in the sun isn't on my agenda. I turn my back on the siren call of the resting spot and fall into step behind Filippo.

A stooped man, his face lined with wrinkles, opens the front door before we can knock. He invites us in without asking our names, clearly expecting us. Filippo asks permission to enter in Italian and the old man, who must be Signor Pavan, waves us onward.

"Prego, prego! Come in."

I match Filippo's movements, slipping off my shoes and leaving them near the door. The deep carpet runner is soft under my feet as we make our way into the house. I do my best to keep up, but a brightly coloured painting catches my eye. The incredible detail calls for a closer inspection. The scene depicts an old-fashioned seaside. Front and centre is a fisherman displaying his daily catch. Nearby, a pair of women in bathing costumes frolic in the sea.

Signor Pavan steps beside me. "You like it, no? It was my wife's favourite painting of mine. Said it made her think of our beach house when the weather was cold and wet."

"Your painting?" I ask, sure I misunderstood.

"Yes, painting is my hobby. My father told me to become a commercialista — an accountant, as you say in English. Said it would pay the bills. But I could not put aside my art entirely."

"You certainly have plenty to inspire you outside your front door."

"That is true!" he agrees with a twinkle in his eye. "My wife's family owned the vineyard. My children and grandchildren now oversee it. They want me to move closer to town, but how could I leave behind such a setting?"

He doesn't wait for an answer to his rhetorical question before motioning me through a doorway into the kitchen. Filippo is already sitting at the table. I take the seat across from him, assuming Signor Pavan will choose the head of the table for himself.

"I get us some caffé and then we talk, okay?" the old man says as he bustles around the kitchen. Within moments, the scent of thick, rich espresso hangs in the air. He pours tiny cups and sets them before us, adding a plate of biscuits to the table before taking his seat.

Filippo gives me a quick look, double-checking I'm still on board with our plan. I tilt my head forward in a nod. The floor is his.

"Signor Pavan, thank you for letting us come to visit you on such short notice."

The old man smiles widely and I can see a hint of the handsome rake he must have been in his younger years. Although his green eyes are rheumy, they convey his genuine pleasure at having two strangers at his table.

"At my age, any visitors are welcome. My friends are spread across the cemeteries and assisted living centres. As long as we aren't meeting beside a tombstone, I'm happy to have the company."

Filippo chuckles at Signor Pavan's blunt sentiment, no doubt accustomed to hearing similar talk from his own family members. I sip my espresso, curious to see what approach Filippo will take in bringing up our questions. What did he mean by coaxing Signor Pavan into telling us what we want to know?

Filippo starts by establishing our bonafides. He spends absolute ages going through a list of shared connections. He might as well get out his family tree and lay it on the table, given how many branches he references without ever getting to the point of why we're here.

I sit quietly and smile harmlessly. My espresso cup runs dry. The biscuits disappear despite my best efforts to nibble slowly. Meanwhile, the Italian men run through a who's who of local residents. Filippo pauses for a breath, giving me a moment of hope. But no, it is only to shift the topic to football, the great Italian pastime. Knowing nothing about the sport, I can't find any way to insert my voice into the conversation.

My smile turns brittle as my patience unravels. When I can take it no more, I fall upon my last resort. Under the table, I use my foot to rap Filippo's leg. Filippo startles at the not-so-gentle nudge, his gaze shooting at me. I raise my eyebrows, letting my facial expression convey my frustration with our progress. When

I notice Signor Pavan looking my way, I hurriedly smooth my grimace into a grin.

While Filippo is struggling to figure out how to react to his partner's unorthodox intervention, Signor Pavan takes the hint.

"Scusi, Ms Payne. We men can talk about sports until we run out of breath. Without my wife here to remind me of my social niceties, I get carried away. I assume you have some reason for your visit. Perhaps we should move the discussion on to more relevant topics."

"Grazie,"I reply, taking care to roll the r. "Shall I start with an explanation for why we're here?" When Signor Pavan nods, I continue. I stick as close to the truth as I can, since I can't depend on the magic of Oxford to smooth over any concerns he might have.

"Since Oxford and Padua are now twin cities, I wanted to take advantage of the opportunity to get to know more about the local people. It will help me come up with more ideas about how we can connect the two cultures. My colleague introduced me to Lavinia. After meeting her family, I was intrigued to learn more about her Great-aunt Angelina. You won't believe this, but my dear friend Harry is the spitting image of her! I asked if I could speak to some people who knew Angelina well. Given how long ago she died, the list was rather short."

"Sandra told you about me?" Paolo asks, referring to Lavinia's mum. "I was always amazed that she never told her mother about what she saw that day. No point keeping it a secret now. Anyone who could be hurt is dead."

Filippo subtly shifts position. His interest is as peaked as mine.

"I was in love with Angelina. She felt the same way about me, although she was loath to admit it. She was older than I was, and I think that embarrassed her. I didn't care one whit about it, but she worried people would talk." Signor Pavan looks upward, lost in his memories. "I asked her to marry me many times, but she always said no. Said I should find someone closer to my own age who could give me children. Don't get me wrong, I love my family. But at the time, I'd have given up that future for a chance to spend the rest of my life with Angelina."

"Where were you when she died?" Filippo asks.

"I was in Padova. We'd made plans to go away for the weekend. It was the middle of the summer, and most everyone was away at the beach. We were going to head south, far from anyone we knew. It took me ages to convince her to do it. But I thought that if we had one normal weekend together — a few days of seeing what our life would be like — I knew she'd come around and accept my proposal."

I don't have to fake the tears that spring to my eyes. I reach over and lay a hand on his wrinkled one. "Why didn't you tell her family about you two? Why keep the secret? It must have been hard to mourn by yourself."

Signor Pavan gives me a grateful smile. "I half-hoped Sandra would tell someone, freeing me from my promise to keep our love affair a secret. The family had enough to grieve without me unveiling hidden truths. What good would it have done them to learn she'd been in love and hadn't felt comfortable enough to share it with them?"

My heart grows heavy at his words. He made the right call, but even now I can see how much it pained him to keep it to himself. I decide to take a risk.

"Signor Pavan, did you ever think her death might not have been an accident?"

The old man's head snaps up, his eyes rimmed in red. "What? No! Why would you ask that?"

I shrug apologetically. "Lavinia's nonna said Angelina had been seeing another man. I think she said his name was Marco. Maybe Marco was angry or hurt?"

The tension bleeds from Signor Pavan's shoulders. "Marco Zanardi, that's who she meant. There is no way he'd have been angry or hurt. It's not my place to explain why, but trust me. He was one of the few who knew about my relationship with Angelina."

Filippo steps into the conversation, drawing Signor Pavan's attention to his side of the table. I paste on a bland smile while I turn his answer over in my head. Marco is dead. Why does Signor Pavan feel the need to keep his secrets?

Unfortunately, I can't pry, not without a good reason or solid evidence he isn't telling the truth. I park the idea there, hoping my friends will find something useful. Right now, I've got questions with no answers.

In short order, we wrap up our visit and gather our things, retracing our steps to the door. Before we leave, Filippo turns back with one final question.

It's the last thing I expect him to ask.

"Signor Pavan, have you ever seen a ghost?"

"A ghost?" The old man's eyebrows skyrocket. "I'm old, but I'm not senile. The only people who come around here are very much alive."

Filippo glances over his shoulder, giving me a satisfied smirk.

However, Signor Pavan isn't done talking.

"If you ask me if I believe in ghosts... that would get you a different answer. Things happen which we can't explain. For example, every time my glasses go missing, I always find them on the kitchen table."

Filippo waits for a beat before suggesting, "Because you always leave them there?"

Signor Pavan chuckles, his shoulders rolling in laughter. "The kitchen table is the first and last place I look, but they're never there until the second time I pass. I know it is my wife taking care of me. She did the same thing when she was alive. She'd come across my glasses wherever I abandoned them, and she'd return them to the table for me to find later."

Filippo is gob smacked. Signor Pavan slaps him on the arm. "Don't be so quick to dismiss things you haven't experienced. You're young yet, there's still plenty of time."

I wisely keep my mouth shut. Signor Pavan said everything I wanted. I couldn't have put it more eloquently if I'd tried.

Chapter Twelve

The conversation with Signor Pavan sheds no light on the mystery. It does, however, give me a couple of ideas of things to look into next. On the drive back to Padua, Filippo suggests we see how the others are getting along. I open the group chat on my phone and see that they have already organised a lunch catch up.

Filippo's mobile rings with a call from the station. He asks if I mind if he puts it on speakerphone, only answering once I've assured him it is fine. With lunch arrangements in place and Filippo occupied, I'm free to turn my attention toward other things, namely writing as much as I can remember of what Signor Pavan said.

I eschew my typical list in favour of a winding path of doodles. It helps me to remember the discussion as though it were a roadway. My brain latches onto the points where I wish I'd taken a turn and prodded for more information. To anyone else, my notes page looks like a mess of scribble. But for my dyslexic brain, there is no better way to review.

My memory runs dry as we turn into the now familiar streets of the centre of Padua. By the time we find a parking space, I barely have time to run by the rental flat to pick up the things I'll need for the afternoon. With Filippo's expert guidance to prevent me from getting lost, we arrive at the restaurant at the same time as the others.

The day has warmed up, and there is a steady flow of people walking through the piazzas. Lavinia commandeers a trio of tables under the cover of a portico, drags them together, and hands us each a menu. The arched overhang protects us from birds flying overhead, while H's fiery breath warns off any pigeons who dare to venture close to our feet.

H leaps into the chair at the head of our table, and suggests Mathilde and me sit on his right and left.

Lavinia slides into the chair beside Mathilde. Filippo looks over the options and chooses the chair farthest from H. That's fine with me. It gives me the ideal position to keep an eye on Filippo. I'm curious to know what he took away from our morning assignment. In due course, a waiter appears to take our orders. Mathilde and I pick large salads, for a change, and I tag on an order for a margarita pizza for H.

Filippo wrinkles his brow as I place my order. "I've never seen anyone order a pizza for their cat."

H, fumes. Literally.

"You've never seen a cat that turns into a wyvern. You could though," I add. "All you have to do is take H's paw in one hand and mine in another."

H lifts a paw in offering but lowers it again when Filippo bursts out laughing.

"I still cannot believe how well you've trained the cat to respond to certain words."

Sensing H's rising fury, Matilde leans over and strokes his scaly forehead. "Don't listen to the bad man, H. If he is too pigheaded to see reason, there's nothing we can do about it."

This time everyone else laughs while Filippo looks like he's swallowed a lemon.

In between bites of food, Mathilde and Harry go first with their update.

"There are crates and trunks galore up there," Mathilde gushes. "I could open a vintage shop just with what we've seen so far. We've barely scratched the surface."

"I'm more of a modern woman, but even I can admit to squealing in delight when I found a box of Pucci scarves." Harry sighs wistfully. "If only they didn't all smell like smoke. Mathilde and I had to take breaks to get some fresh air. H was the only one who could stomach the odour."

"After all these years I'm surprised they still smell," Lavinia admits.

"Angelina's things have been packed away and left untouched," Harry explains. "If they'd been aired out instead of folded up, they would be in better condition."

Kate motions for Harry to move the conversation on to more relevant topics. "Don't keep us in suspense. Did you find anything?"

"Maybe, but hold on to your enthusiasm for a moment. It took us most of the morning to sort through the contents. We pushed anything we thought was relevant off to one side of the attic. There are some boxes of letters and a couple of diaries." Harry glances at me. "Nat and I have a meeting this afternoon. Can you and Lavinia give Mathilde and H a hand going through the written materials?"

"That suits me," Kate answers. She turns to Lavinia and asks, "Do you want to provide our update?"

"Certo! The library staff digitalised the newspaper archives a few years ago, so it didn't take us long to comb through them. We printed off anything we thought might be relevant." Lavinia shifts so we can see the bag hanging from her chair. Sticking out from the top is an oversized red plastic envelope.

"Can you give us some ideas about what you found?" I ask.

Lavinia nods. "Zia Angelina was quite the society darling. There were dozens of photos of her at events. We printed all of those plus some from after her death, which included Marco."

"What about Paulo Pavan? Was he in any of them?"

"If he was, his name wasn't listed," Lavinia answers with a shrug. "I've never met him. Maybe now that you have, you'll spot him in the background."

"On that note," Harry interrupts, "how did your interrogation go?"

I glance at Filippo, but he waves me on, likely curious to see what I thought. In between bites, I run the team through a quick recap, excluding Filippo's lengthy chitchat that started us off.

"It doesn't sound like you got much out of him," Mathilde groans. "He's our only living connection outside of Lavinia's family. I had high hopes he'd provide a clue."

"I'm not so sure that he didn't." I retrieve my notepad and flip to the relevant page. "His story tugged on the heartstrings, but he definitely glossed over the details in some sections."

"You could hardly expect the man to share his intimate secrets with a pair of strangers," Filippo argues.

"I'm not complaining. In some ways, he said more than I expected. However, there were a few offhand remarks which, in retrospect, I should have queried."

Filippo leans back in his chair and levels his gaze on my notes. "Let's hear them."

I point to the circled note near the top of my page. "The first thing that caught my attention was something he said at the start of our conversation. I wouldn't have been surprised if he'd denied the connection between himself and Angelina. But he dived right into the topic, saying he might as well talk about his relationship with Angelina because anyone who could be hurt by it was long dead." I glance up to check my friend's faces before explaining, "We know Angelina kept their relationship a secret, but his phrasing made me think he meant someone else beyond just her."

"Maybe he meant Marco," Lavinia offers, thinking back on her research.

"Good guess, but he said that Marco was one of the few who knew about his relationship with Angelina."

"You think Signor Pavan had his own reason for keeping quiet," Filippo guesses. "His phrasing didn't strike me at the time, but now that I think back on it, I can see your point. Maybe he meant Angelina's family."

"Maybe, but Lavinia's mum knew about their relationship. He had no way of knowing she'd continue to keep it a secret. I should have dug deeper, but his emotional tale of not wanting to burden Angelina's family distracted me. It was so altruistic, and the picture of him mourning her all alone encouraged my emotions to overpower my logic."

"What else have you got on your notepad?" Filippo asks as he leans over the table.

"While you were driving, I asked myself why else Signor Pavan would hide their relationship. We know Angelina continued to go to events with Marco to keep anyone from suspecting her attention was elsewhere. But what about Signor Pavan? I don't know about you, but I don't know many men who would let the love of their life pretend to date someone else. Not unless he was worried about hurting someone in his own life."

Mathilde straightens up and rubs her hands together. "Now we're getting somewhere. If we can figure out who Signor Pavan was hiding the relationship from, we might find a suspect."

The waiter returns to see if we want a coffee or a dessert, reminding me and Harry that we are pressed for time. Meeting or not, I don't want to leave until we've nailed down our next steps.

"Harry and I will have to leave in ten minutes if we want to make it on time. Do you want me to have a look at the photos you printed before I go? Filippo, do you have time to look at a few?"

"I can spare a few more minutes before I need to get to the station," he agrees, showing a newfound willingness to be involved. Our gazes meet from across the table, his mouth turning up in a hint of a smile. Without needing to say a word, his expression reveals his grudging respect for me as a partner.

Lavinia opens the clasp on the folder and divides a stack of print-outs in half, handing part to me and the rest to Filippo. Mathilde swaps seats with H so she can watch as I go through them.

"You weren't kidding about Angelina's involvement in society activities. There are photos from the opera, charity events..." I flip through another couple of pages, reading the notes Lavinia helpfully added below each photo. "The question is, where did she meet Signor Pavan?"

"At an art gallery," Filippo answers. All eyes turn his way to see him waving a photo in the air. "He's here, in the background, standing off to Angelina's left. I don't think he knew he was in the shot, as he appears to be talking to someone out of the frame."

Indeed, a smiling Angelina stands next to the man identified as Marco Zanardi. Both of them hold glasses of bubbly prosecco as they smile for the photographer.

"Of course! Signor Pavan told us he was an artist," I explain for the benefit of the others. "Even if he never sold his work, it would make sense he'd attend art events."

I flip through the remaining pages, looking for any labelled as art or museum or gallery. "Here's another one," I cry, clutching the page. This time it is a candid photo, capturing the crowd as they mill around the space. I trace a line from his gaze to where she is standing with a group of women. "They're not together, but you can see Signor Pavan is watching Angelina."

Lavinia takes the printed pages back when Harry tells me it is time for us to go. Before we leave, we review our plans for the afternoon.

"We'll be at Nonna's house. All of us," Lavinia adds. "Kate can help Mathilde and H while I see if Nonna or my mama recognise anyone else in the photos. What about you two? Where's your meeting?"

"The Padua university team is hosting us for a joint-planning session to firm up the Twin City ceremony." I can't stop my mouth from curving into a frown. "The meeting is in the Palazzo Bo."

Mathilde grimaces at my answer. "Whatever you do, don't take your eyes off Harry, not even for a second."

"Don't worry," I reassure her, looping my arm through Harry's. "We'll be glued at the hip."

As Harry and I wend our way along the cobblestone and pavements of Padua's centre, I raise an issue that's being weighing on my mind. "While solving the mystery of Angelina's death has to be our top priority, I'm concerned we're forgetting about our secondary task."

Harry thinks for a second but comes up blank. "What's that?"

"We've got to find at least one more prefect... ideally two more. But where do we start? And is it even smart to bring someone else into our circle right now? What if we put them in danger?"

"The only one who's in the line of fire right now is me," Harry points out.

"For now," I counter. "With a crazed Eternal on the loose, who knows what they will do next? But I still come back to my chief concern. We have no contenders, Harry. Lavinia is perfect for stepping into Kate's role of overseeing the creative elements like artwork and statuary. Where are we going to find someone, in less than a few days, I might add, who can maintain the magical connection between Padua's knowledge and its people?"

Harry doesn't have an answer for me. All she can do is show her support. "Chin up, Nat. We're on our way to a meeting with representatives from departments across the university and the city. We'll keep our eyes open. Maybe someone will stand out."

Harry's suggestion lifts my spirits. "You're right, Harry. Just like always," I add, making her laugh. "I need to have faith that the magic will somehow call the right people to step forward. I should bring this up with Lavinia, too. She clearly knows many people here. If I ask the right question, she might know just the people to tap for the roles."

"Err," Harry hems, looking at me askance. "There is one other option you're forgetting, Nat."

I search my mind but come up blank. I have no idea who she could mean.

"Filippo! We've already told him magic is real. Why not make him a prefect?"

I shake my head in a vehement no. "He can't be a prefect! He doesn't work for the uni, and certainly has zero desire to organise events and ceremonies. While he said he likes books and studying, he spends most of his days chasing criminals. I can't think of a single criterion he meets."

"Are you so sure about those criteria?" Harry asks. "Think back to the original group who discovered the magical field. How many of them were party planners or librarians? Your formal role at the university is one that evolved much later. Don't be so quick to dismiss Filippo."

"I, um," I stumble over my words. Harry has thrown me for a

loop with her excellent point. I should search much more broadly for potential caretakers.

I'm still gnawing over that idea as we arrive at the entrance to the Palazzo Bo. My stomach lurches when I see the front door, my body remembering the stress of my last visit. Even Harry hovers outside, unable to force herself to go any further.

I wish H was with us. He'd make some off-the-wall comment about slow-roasting our enemies or something similar, cajoling a laugh from us at just the right moment. Since he isn't here, it falls to me.

My mind goes blank when I search for a funny quip. The memory of the woman lying there, dead for all I knew, wipes all humour from my head. All I can conjure up is a speech steeped in honesty.

I pull Harry to the side and angle my body so I can look her in the eye. "I'm scared, Harry. I don't want to go back in there. I bet you share my trepidation. Perhaps now is a good time for both of us to remember that we're not alone. We've got each other, plus our friends, and whatever helpful Eternals linger in these halls." I squeeze Harry's hand. "Can we do this?"

Harry releases the breath she'd been holding in. "We can, Nat. We are compelled to see this through to the end."

Once more infused with determination, Harry rolls her shoulders back, tilts her head from side to side, loosening her neck, and marches through the entrance.

Inside the building, bland, everyday activities surround us. A man hurries past, clutching a stack of papers against his chest. A trio of young students huddles in a corner of the room, laughing at a joke. Behind the information desk, a competent staff directs visitors and answers questions. Faced with so much normalcy, the last of my worries fades away.

"Oh look, there's the Vice-Chancellor's PA," Harry murmurs, pointing towards a short, balding man standing on the far side of the room. She waves hello and he motions for us to follow him. It only takes a moment for us to catch up. I keep Harry positioned in between myself and the man. It might be silly, but I can't help wanting to protect her.

After several minutes of walking through narrow hallways lined with doors, we end up in a large conference room. Twenty smiling faces turn our way as we enter the space. Harry and I squeeze into the only empty chairs around the oval table, the last to arrive despite being on time.

The session starts off well, with us taking turns to introduce ourselves and explain our role. I take copious notes of who everyone is, just in case anyone stands out as a potential candidate for a prefect role. We settle in as one of the Italians gives a presentation of the existing plans for the twinning ceremony, and wraps up with a list of items still open for discussion.

From there, the meeting enters a deathly downward spiral. The discussion is an unmitigated disaster. Not because of any cross-cultural communications problems, but because the Italians can't agree amongst themselves. There are too many departments represented, each with its own vision for the event. Every item devolves into a heated debate. Should we be indoors or outside? Who will stand where? Will the ceremony have more impact if they speak in Latin?

Our little cohort of Oxonians doesn't stand a chance. I switch from making notes about the people to devising ever more elaborate escape ideas. Just as I'm ready to sneak out and pull the fire alarm, someone finally notices the time and calls the meeting to an end.

We stand to leave, and I'm amazed at the smiles on the faces of the Italians. They don't seem bothered in the least. If anything, they're even more energised. I wonder whether I missed something, and lean close to Harry to ask, "Were you as miserable and frustrated as I was?"

She gives me a wide-eyed look of agreement, equally shellshocked by ups and downs of the Italians' search for a compromise. "They talked for the whole afternoon! I don't think we said more than three words after the introductions!"

I glance at my watch and am shocked to see how late it is. As desperate as I am to get out of here, all the water I sipped during the session is having an impact. Harry agrees to a quick pop to the loo before we leave. After getting directions to the nearest one, we say our goodbyes and sneak off from the group.

The closest bathroom ends up being up a floor at the end of another long hallway. Our footsteps are the only sounds. Behind the frosted glass doors, the rooms are dark and empty. By unspoken agreement, we hurry as fast as we can. As I'm drying my hands, I hear a door slam shut.

I'd like to believe it is someone else wandering around. But no footsteps follow the bang.

"Maybe it was the wind?" My voice trembles.

Harry shoves the strap of her handbag higher up her shoulder and hardens her expression. I know that look. It is her take-no-prisoners face.

"Let's go, Nat," she intones in a low voice. There's no space for argument.

I gulp.

She pushes open the door and strides into the hallway. Every other light is out, making a checkerboard on the floor.

Harry doesn't linger. She makes a beeline for the stairwell at the end of the hall. I stay so close, I'm practically glued to her heels.

A doorknob jiggles, followed by a creak. I tell myself not to look back, but that only makes it worse. I throw a glance over my shoulder in time to see a book flying through the air, aiming straight for my head.

"Duck!" I shout, pulling Harry sideways. The book skims over our heads and ricochets off the wall.

Further ahead in the corridor, another door clicks open. Harry and I lock eyes as we wrap our hands around our handbag straps. We take off in a sprint.

We dodge a canal of projectiles. More books fly past. A metal stapler lands with an awful clatter. I throw up a hand to block a pair of scissors. The sharp edge slices across my palm.

Where is H with his magic-revealing collar when we need him? This would be a lot simpler if we could see who we are up against. Has the hall grown twice as long? It certainly seems that way by the time we reach the fire door marking the stairwell. Harry shoves on the handlebar. It doesn't give.

We're trapped!

Harry bangs on the door, pleading for help.

Behind us, silence hangs in the air. Like the calm in the middle of a hurricane, I know it is only a brief reprieve. Angelina's killer is gearing up for one last strike.

With no options left, Harry and I turn, putting our backs against the door. We stare down the hallway, practically daring the spirit to do its worst.

If only we had a clue how to defend ourselves.

Right then, the door opens.

The fire door. It swings wide and I have to catch myself on the doorjamb to keep from falling backwards into the stairwell landing.

My brain can't process fast enough.

"What are you two doing?" Filippo asks, incredulous at the sight of me and Harry so dishevelled and sweaty.

My breath is coming out too fast to allow space for words. All I can do is point toward the hallway. Other than a couple of books and few office supplies littering the floor, there is no sign of our attacker.

I stutter through an explanation, raising Filippo's eyebrows. He tells us to stand still and then marches onto the battleground. He checks every door, poking his head inside each room. But, of course, there's nothing there for him to see. Even we couldn't see our ghostly attacker.

"There's no one here," he announces when he again reaches our side.

Harry inhales and I know she's gearing up for a blistering retort about his unwillingness to accept that we're telling the truth. As much as I agree with her, I know there's no point. We're better off letting the idea linger in his mind, rather than opening a debate on the existence of magic.

I step into the fray, cutting her off before she can start. "What are you doing here? How did you know where to find us?"

"Lavinia asked me to collect you two, and the reception desk staff said I'd likely find you up here." He holds the door open, silently encouraging us to get a move on.

He doesn't have to ask us twice. We make it back to the piazza outside in record time. Filippo guides us to a side road and asks us to wait while he retrieves the car.

As I watch him walk along the pavement, one thing becomes crystal clear. Even Harry can't argue when I point out this truth.

"Filippo can't be a prefect so long as he refuses to accept that magic exists."

Chapter Thirteen

Filippo drops us outside Nonna's house, explaining that the others are waiting for us inside. When I ask why he isn't staying, he replies, "I promised my wife I'd be home for dinner."

As much as I want to demand he stick around for our discussions, I have to give him full credit for knowing his priorities. If he knew my hand was bleeding, he might make a different choice. But since the cut isn't deep enough to warrant more than a bandage, I keep quiet.

Lavinia buzzes the garden gate open as soon as Harry rings the bell, and waits for us on her grandmother's front porch.

"Is everything okay?" Harry asks. "Filippo didn't explain why we were meeting here when he dropped us off."

"Everything is fine," Lavinia reassures us. "The others are still in the attic, combing through the last trunks and boxes. Nonna offered to feed us, and since her cooking is better than mine and she doesn't have any small children to get in our way, I took her up on it."

As we're divesting ourselves of our jackets and bags, Lavinia notices the blood-stained tissue I'm holding.

"Nat! You're hurt! What happened?"

Harry spins around, also caught off-guard. She'd ridden in the front seat with Filippo and hadn't noticed my covert efforts to address the cut in my hand. "You're bleeding? Why didn't you say something? Did you get hurt during our escape?"

"Escape?!" Lavinia's screech echoes in the front hallway. I rush to shush her, not wanting to attract her nonna's attention.

"It's barely more than a scratch," I promise, pulling away the tissue to expose the angry red line across my palm.

Lavinia levels me with a stern gaze. "I'll get the first aid kit. Why don't you two head on up?" she suggests, pointing to the stairs. "But don't start the story until I get there. I don't want to miss a word."

Harry's disapproving glare lets me know she's thinking the same thing. "You should have told me you got hurt," she says in a harsh whisper. My explanation of not wanting to make Filippo feel obligated to remain only somewhat mollifies her.

Nonna's attic turns out to be a series of storage rooms on the third floor of the house. H flaps into the hallway when he hears footsteps on the stairs.

"Lor luv a duck, Nat! What 'appened to your 'and?" H swoops in for a closer look, nearly bumping into Harry.

Harry rolls her eyes and waves him back into the room with the others. "Give Lavinia a minute to catch up and we'll tell you."

In short order, I find myself seated on an old chair crammed between piles of boxes. The white sheet tossed over it for protection prevents me from discovering the broken springs until they poke into my back. That annoyance pales compared to the bolt of pain that runs up my arm when Lavinia pours pure rubbing alcohol over my wound.

Harry notes my gritted teeth and takes that as her cue to update Kate, Mathilde, Lavinia, and H about our eventful afternoon.

She begins with the obvious. "We were attacked! It felt like a scene from a horror movie."

"How?" Mathilde blurts.

"Where?" Kate adds. "Was anyone else around?"

Harry tells them to calm down and she'll answer all their questions. "We were on our own, in the Palazzo Bo. The meeting had lasted for hours, going around and around in circles. Nat and I were at our wit's end by the time it wrapped up. I guess that's why we let our guard down. We asked for directions to the loo and ended up on an empty floor."

"I still can't believe how fast the ghost moved around. It leapt from one office to another, sending doors flying open and then slinging projectiles at our heads. This cut," I add, holding my injured hand in the air. "It came from a pair of scissors."

"We finally reached the door to the stairwell, but the ghost was still a step ahead of us. The handle refused to budge. We're lucky Filippo showed up when he did." Harry pauses, struck by a wayward thought. "Wait, was that a coincidence?"

Lavinia, white as a sheet, shakes her head. "I felt this incredible urge to phone him and ask him to give you a ride. He was passing right by the Palazzo when I rang."

"It seems the Eternals are doing their best to offer us some protection, whichever way they can. I bet Elena Cornaro was involved. She's based in the Palazzo Bo and probably spotted the wayward Eternal spying on us." I rock back in amazement and get poked by a broken spring. "There's no telling how long Angelina's killer was following us around. They must have kept a close eye in order to attack at just the right moment."

My friends all nod their agreement with my sentiments. It goes unsaid that the Eternal could be watching us even now. There's no point in travelling down that path — there's nothing we can do to prevent them from staying close. Our best defence is to solve this mystery as soon as we can.

"How about you? Did you find anything in Angelina's old stuff?" I grasp the size of the challenge as I look around me for the first time, taking in the sheer volume of items stored in the top floor rooms.

"It's not as bad as it seems at first glance," Mathilde reassures me, catching the look on my face. "A few minutes before you arrived we found two letters... or, I should say, H found two letters."

"And to think, Filippo doubted your ability to read Italian," I say, giving my cheeky wyvern a thumb's up.

"There was a problem," H admits, shuffling his taloned feet on the hardwood floor. "When I realised what I was reading, I felt a nervous sneeze coming on."

Mathilde chimes in before I can worry. "I was right beside him. When I caught sight of him rearing back his snout, sniffling and snorting, I wrapped a hand around his mouth and blocked him mid-sneeze."

"You're lucky you weren't injured." I wave my hurt hand in the air. "We could have been in the sick ward together."

"Ha! I wasn't sure whether H's magical collar would be enough to repair the letters like it would do in Oxford. I don't even want to think about what his fire might do to my hand." Mathilde shivers in mock-horror, making us all laugh with her.

Harry coughs politely, calling us back to attention. "Where are the letters? What's in them?"

Lavinia pulls two pieces of paper from a stack at her side and smoothes them with her hand. "I'll start by saying they aren't signed, and we don't have any way to identify the sender. But they are handwritten, so at least that's something. The letters are brief, but impactful. The sender all but begs Angelina to give up her relationship, for the good of all involved."

I wait a beat, expecting more information, but Lavinia has

nothing left to add. "Which relationship? The one with Marco or the one with Paolo Pavan?"

She shrugs, just as mystified. "We found the letters shoved into her diary, close to the day she died. They were mixed in with a bill from the same time period, so I assume she received them in the week or so before her death."

"Now you see why I sneezed, Missie," H quips, his yellow eyes glowing with pride. "I took one look at the words on that letter and knew I 'ad found a clue!"

"You did good," I answer. I turn to Lavinia and ask, "Do you think you can spare an extra portion of parmesan as a reward?"

"At the bare minimum! I'd almost given up hope. Now that we have a clue, what do we do with it? Should we call Filippo?"

"We could... but I suspect there is someone even more qualified. Signor Pavan — he must know something more than he's told us so far. I walked away from my meeting with him feeling like he'd held information back. This is exactly the proof I need to convince him to loosen his lips."

"Do you think he'll tell you everything this go around?"

I ponder Lavinia's question and don't like where I end up. "Maybe?" I shrug. "I guess it all comes down to why he is holding onto these secrets in the first place. Is he honouring someone's final wishes or covering up for a friend? Those two reasons could lead to very different outcomes."

"That's the truth," Mathilde grumbles. She's sitting in the middle of a pile of old clothes, lounging against the side of a leather-covered trunk. With her floral t-shirt and jeans, she almost looks like she could be an Eternal from the 1970s.

Kate, on the other hand, shows little sign of the afternoon spent digging through Nonna's attic. Her trousers still have a perfect crease running down the front. But I know her well enough to recognise the rolled-up sleeves and scarf tied around her hair as indicators that she's hard at work. Kate ignores the weight of my stare, lost in her own thoughts.

"What's going through your head, Kate? Maybe it will help if you talk it out."

"I was thinking about how you've got people to come clean in the past, Nat. Often you'd have some clue or key piece of information or something else to use as leverage. We've got the letters, but we don't know enough about the writer to be able to wield them as a weapon against him. What's stopping him from saying he doesn't recognise the handwriting and doesn't know what they are about?"

"If we could let him see Angelina, or somehow get a glimpse of his past..." Mathilde murmurs, half under her breath.

"Wait a minute," Lavinia interrupts, her voice tinged with excitement. "What if we got my nonna to help us? If she invited Signor Pavan here, and showed him some of Angelina's old photos and personal items, it's bound to trigger some nostalgia. Under those circumstances, if she asked him about the letters, I think he'd have a very hard time looking her in the eye and telling her he knows nothing about them."

Harry raises one finger to highlight a question. "It's a good play, but it would require you to tell your nonna what we're doing. Are you sure you want to risk reopening an old wound?"

Lavinia doesn't hesitate. "I've always known I'd have to tell Nonna what we're doing. You can't live as long as she has without figuring out when someone is up to something. The only reason she's given us free rein up here is because she knows I'll confess everything when the time is right. And that time is now." She rises from where she's sitting on the floor in front of me. "Come on. We can all go. And bring the letters."

We make enough ruckus going down the two flights of stairs to give Nonna plenty of warning. When we reach the ground floor, she's standing in the doorway of the sitting room.

"Nonna, possiamo parlarti?" Lavinia asks. Her grandmother gives a single nod of agreement and then turns around and disappears into the sitting room. By the time I come in last, she's found the remote and is turning off the television.

Nonna claims her leather lounger, leaning back to prop up her feet. Lavinia takes the closest seat at the end of the sofa, with Kate and Harry filling in next to her. Mathilde and I opt for a pair of wooden chairs, while H curls at my feet.

"Okay, Lavinia mia, are you ready to tell me what you and your friends are up to in my attic?"

"Sí, Nonna," Lavinia replies, barely holding back a laugh. Slowly, she recounts the story of Harry's misadventures and our discovery of her resemblance to Angelina. Although Lavinia keeps the existence of magic a secret, she hints at an otherworldly element. Nonna doesn't bat an eyelid when Lavinia suggests a ghost is haunting Harry. She does, however, sit up straight when Lavinia passes her the letters H found.

We hold our breath as she skims the two pages, waiting for her pronouncement. When Nonna glances up at us again, her cheeks are pink with rage.

"Someone hurt Angelina? They threatened her? Over a man? Why? Why would they do such a thing?"

Lavinia reaches over and grips her grandmother's hand tight. "I don't know, but I intend to find out. Do you recognise the handwriting? Or know which man they refer to?"

Nonna is mystified. "None of this is familiar, Lavinia. I thought Angelina had a nice arrangement with Marco. But then your mamma brought up Signor Pavan, and now you tell me that it was true. Angelina was seeing him in secret. I would like to know myself what these mean."

Harry leans forward until she catches Nonna's eye. "We need your help getting Signor Pavan to tell us what he knows. Angelina was your sister. I can't imagine he could look you in the face and lie, especially if you ask him a direct question."

Nonna looks again at the letters, her hand trembling. "I will never be able to rest until I know I've got justice for my sister. If Paolo Pavan knows something, he won't leave this house until he tells it all."

Although I'm thrilled with Nonna's fiery sense of justice, I can't help feel somewhat sorry for Signor Pavan. The poor old man has no idea what he's up against. The only thing worse than having an amateur sleuth on your trail is facing the fury of a woman with nothing left to lose.

❖

Despite our sense of urgency, the earliest Nonna can arrange for Signor Pavan to visit is the next day. He gratefully accepts Nonna's invitation to dinner and shows no surprise when she mentions I'll also be there. He's keen to meet Harry, the woman who looks so much like the once love-of-his-life.

At precisely seven in the evening, the doorbell rings. Lavinia and I rush off to answer it, leaving the rest of our friends to finish setting the table in Nonna's dining room. Even Filippo has turned up for the event, equally intrigued by the discovery of the letters.

Signor Pavan is using a cane to keep him steady, a slender wooden rod with no frippery or decoration. His sparse white hair has been carefully combed and smoothed in place. I can't help but smile as he takes the hand I offer and bows over it.

"Signorina, we meet again," he says smoothly, giving me a knowing look. "I suspected you might pass along some of our conversation to Lavinia's family. The only thing which took me by surprise was how quickly Carlotta got in touch."

"I'm fifty years late," Lavinia's grandmother retorts after swapping cheek kisses with the old man. "Or I should say that you are late. So many times we saw each other over the years and you never gave even a hint that you shared a deeper connection with me."

Signor Pavan has the grace to blush, turning pink under the age spots on his weathered and lined cheeks. "Ahh, Carlotta. What can I say? It was too soon to impose my grief upon yours and then too late to bring it up. If there was a right moment in time to tell you everything, it slipped past me."

Lavinia smoothly steps into their discussion, fixing Signor Pavan with a serious look. "Water under the bridge, Signor Pavan. All that matters is that we're here now and can finally be honest with one another. Completely honest," she adds.

Lavinia and I take the lead as we return to the others, leaving him and Nonna to ask after each other's families and shared friends.

At the doorway to the dining room, Nonna pauses and motions for Signor Pavan to proceed her. "Come, meet the rest of my guests."

Harry sits on the far side of the room, positioned so as not to immediately draw his eye. It's of no use. He skims right past Mathilde and Kate, searching the room until he spots Harry.

"Dio mio," he gasps. He trembles as though he's seeing a ghost.

Harry, ever the kind-heart, leaps from her chair and strides around the table to join him. "Hello Mr Pavan," she says, her English accent heavier than ever. "I'm Harriet Dalrymple. It's a pleasure to meet you."

Harry's voice and words break the spell that seems to have entranced Signor Pavan. He shakes it off, and remembering himself, returns her introduction with his own greeting.

"What do you think, Paolo?" Lavinia's nonna asks. "Is she Angelina's identical twin?"

I freeze in place, hearing the unspoken test in Nonna's

question. It had taken her seconds to spot all the differences between Harry and Angelina. Paolo Pavan's answer will prove how well he truly knew her sister.

Paolo fumbles a pair of glasses from his shirt pocket and shoves them onto his face. His eyes are comically large behind the lens, making it easy to see how his gaze narrows as he scans Harry's face.

"Molto simile," he begins, "but her nose is straight. I remember Angelina having a small bump halfway down. And her eye colour is not the same."

Nonna smiles as Signor Pavan's answer puts any doubts to rest. "Angelina fractured her nose while skipping rope."

"She told me," he echoes. "Said her feet got tangled, and she was so worried about protecting her new dress that she forgot to guard her face." He and Nonna both chuckle at the memory.

We make quick work of explaining who the others are, and then we take our seats. Harry remains at the far end of the table, acting as a subtle reminder of why we're gathered together. Nonna sits at the head, with Paolo Pavan on her right and Lavinia on her left. Filippo helps himself to the chair next to Signor Pavan, likely thinking the men should stick together. Kate and I fill into the remaining seats beside Lavinia, while Mathilde sits between Filippo and Harry. I'd chosen my seat so I'd be able to keep a close eye on Signor Pavan's expression throughout the meal.

Filippo does the honours of opening the wine while Nonna's housekeeper brings in steaming plates of spaghetti with clams. I cast a quick glance at H, who's innocently curled in a chair in the corner of the room. He looks every inch the tranquil domestic feline, as long as you can't see the tendril of smoke coming from his nostril.

He winks one yellow eye at me, letting me know he is okay. He should be, considering the quantity of pasta he ate before

Signor Pavan arrived. We didn't want anything to distract Signor Pavan when it comes time to ask him our questions.

Over dinner, Nonna and Paolo Pavan reminisce about their youthful adventures and escapades in Padua and its surroundings. Lavinia and Filippo encourage them anytime the conversation lags. As fellow locals, they're clearly enjoying the topic as much as the older people.

After the main course of fish and grilled vegetables is served, Paolo Pavan shifts the discussion to our end of the table. He asks questions about our background and how we all met. He can hardly believe it when he hears how long Kate and Lavinia have been friends. Harry utterly charms him, and not only because of her resemblance to Angelina. She's had years of High Table dinners at the college to perfect her technique of conversing with strangers.

If I didn't know what else we had planned for the evening, the meal would be a delight. But with every spoonful of ice cream I eat for dessert, my shoulders grow tight with nerves. We're so close to finding out the truth. Will Signor Pavan finally come clean with the whole story?

Nonna waits until the last plate is cleared from the table and everyone has a thimble-sized glass of grappa. Only then, when the last social nicety has been properly observed, does she steer the conversation towards our area of interest.

"Lavinia, will you bring me the photos you found?"

Lavinia does as her grandmother bids and collects a stack of old photographs from a nearby drawer. She passes them into her grandmother's outstretched hand. There aren't many of them, but each one was carefully selected to elicit a response.

"The girls have been going through Angelina's things and discovered these tucked away. I thought you might like to see them. We'll start with my favourite." Nonna hands the top photo to Signor Pavan. "Based on my recollection, this one must have been taken shortly before her death. I thought you might have been the photographer."

Paolo Pavan pulls his glasses out again and studies the print. "This is exactly as I remember her. So vibrant and full of life." He holds the photo up so we can see. The picture captures a woman with her head thrown back, her mouth open in what can only be laughter. It's the type of expression which cannot be faked. Her hair is longer than Harry's and her profile is slightly different. However, I've seen Harry laugh that way enough times to be able to imagine the scene.

"I asked Angelina to give me this photo, but she refused. It was her only copy, a gift from Rosa," he adds.

Nonna passes the next photo over. It's an event photo showing Angelina and Marco. "I never understood why Angelina and Marco didn't settle down together. Were you the reason?"

Again, Signor Pavan shakes his head. "I told Natalie the truth. Marco had given us his blessing."

"Why would he do that? He seemed to genuinely care about Angelina."

"He did, Carlotta, very much so. He adored Angelina, and she felt the same about him. In the beginning, I was terribly jealous of their friendship. Marco came to see me one day. He knew how much I loved Angelina, but he also understood her reasons for keeping our relationship hidden. He offered to trade his secret for ours. He would tell me the truth about himself, and in exchange, I would let him parade Angelina at events and provide her with a cover story."

Nonna stares, struck silent by his words. Lavinia steps in to the gap. "What was his secret? Surely you can tell us. Whatever it was, it can't harm him now."

Signor Pavan swallows, his Adam's apple bobbing in his wrinkled neck. "You young people won't understand, but Carlotta, I know you will. Times were different back then. He'd have been shunned by society if they knew where his heart truly lay."

My brain fumbles to understand what he is saying. Harry gets there faster than I do.

"Marco was gay?"

"Yes. Angelina wouldn't have betrayed him for anything. If he hadn't told me himself, I think she would have broken things off with me rather than reveal his secret."

It takes Nonna a moment to square this truth against the man she knew. She must have known Marco well, given her close relationship with her sister. She looks at the remaining photographs in her gnarled hands, judging where to go next. After a beat, she sets the stack aside, instead sliding a hand into her dress pocket. She retrieves the letters we found in Angelina's diary.

"You talk of Angelina's friends, but I notice you don't mention any enemies. But I know she had at least one. We found these shoved inside a book, mixed in with bills from the month before her death. What do you make of them?"

Signor Pavan is perplexed as Nonna hands him the papers. He squints at the writing, moving his hand until he has the paper in just the right spot. No one else moves.

Every eye in the room is fixed on Signor Pavan. Even H has sat up on his chair and angled his body until he has a clear view.

Signor Pavan's mouth moves silently as he reads the words scrawled across the page, his breath rasping. He looks at one page and then another, flipping them over to check both sides.

When he looks up, his eyes are rimmed with red.

"Dimmi, Paolo!" Nonna insists, merciless in her attack. "You know something. Who sent these to my sister? Who threatened her?"

"She meant no harm, I swear it..." he mumbles.

"Who!" Nonna demands.

Signor Pavan chokes when he tries to answer. Filippo passes him a glass of water and encourages him to sip slowly. Gradually, Signor Pavan regains control. His voice is steady when he finally replies.

"It's been several years since I've seen it, but I'd know this handwriting anywhere. My wife wrote this. We weren't married at the time," he hastens to add. "I'd been on a few dates with her, mostly to satisfy Angelina's demands that I see other people. Angelina worried I'd regret the decision to sacrifice having children in order to be with her. She insisted I at least explore other options."

I scrunch my brow as I try to understand what he's saying. "If you had only been on a few dates, why would she send notes like this to Angelina? How would she even know you two were together, especially given the lengths you went to in order to keep it a secret?"

Signor Pavan is unfortunately as mystified as the rest of us. "I don't have the faintest clue. Perhaps she saw us together, or followed me one night? I can't explain it."

"But why would she send Angelina a letter instead of confronting you?"

"My wife wasn't the confrontational type. She feared public opinion, and never let her emotions get the better of her when anyone could see. I'm not sure that she meant her words as a threat, so much as a warning to Angelina. We were playing with fire — her and Marco, me and her. My wife was an innocent bystander who simply got swept up in our actions. I never meant to hurt her, to hurt anyone," he emphasises. "But my wife was right. If the truth had come out, all of us would have been exposed to ridicule. Angelina and Marco were darlings of high society. They had excellent reasons for acting as they did, but I don't think society would have stopped to ask them."

My stomach drops at his explanation, mostly because I can

hear the truth in it. Yet, I'm not ready to accept it. I drag my gaze away from Signor Pavan to see how Nonna is reacting.

The old woman lifts a fist to her mouth and stopping a sob before it can slip out. Lavinia leaps to her feet and throws her arms around her grandmother, enveloping her in a hug. Nonna pats her arms and slowly regains control. When she speaks, her voice is raw.

"What fools we were, Paolo. And yes, I am including myself. It must have seemed like such a neat solution when Angelina and Marco made their original agreement. She had no plans to marry again. He needed an escort who was above reproach. Neither of them could have imagined that, of all things, love would rear up and ruin their plans. I was so busy raising children and keeping house, I let my relationship with Angelina grow distant. I always assumed we'd have time later. And then we didn't."

There isn't a dry eye around the table by the time she chokes out her last words. Even Filippo is furiously wiping his eyes.

But one question remains unanswered. Did Signor Pavan's wife take her warning a step further? It makes my heart ache to ask, even though I know I must.

"Signor Pavan, is there any chance that your wife had something to do with Angelina's death?"

He blanches again but doesn't respond badly to my accusation. After a night of discoveries, he accepts that this must be considered. I watch as his eyes shift from left to right while he searches his mind for memories of that fateful day.

His shoulders are tight, and his nerves are fraught. When I can stand it no longer, he exhales in a whoosh. "No, no, no. She could not have done it. She wasn't in Padova. She'd gone away with her family to the beach, near Venice. Punta Sabbioni, to be exact."

I have no idea where that is, but the Italians at the table nod their understanding.

"Getting there, even now, is complicated unless you have a car. Otherwise, you need to change buses, or use the train and then traghetto from Venezia. She couldn't have snuck back to Padova without anyone noticing her absence."

"Could she have driven back?" Lavinia asks, pointing out the one option left on the table.

"She didn't learn to drive a car until we had children. And then, only because I forced her to tackle her fear. She did return to Padova a few days after Angelina's death. My mother called the place where they were staying and told her what had happened. She came home and supported me through my grief. That was when our affection grew. Perhaps it is wishful thinking, but I always thought Angelina had a hand in that. Somehow, her spirit was there, helping me find my way to the future she wanted me to have."

"I'm sure that is exactly what she did," Nonna agrees. "I've felt her spirit near me many times over the years."

While the two older adults share a moment of deep understanding and acceptance, I catch Mathilde's eye. If Signor Pavan's wife isn't our killer, I've got no ideas left of where to find the person who is responsible.

Chapter Fourteen

A night of sleep fails to bring us any fresh ideas on how to identify Angelina's killer. Nonetheless, not a single one of us is willing to sit back and accept defeat. Especially not with Harry's life at risk.

Despite our determination, there is an air of dejectedness hanging over our rental flat. I can practically hear the clock ticking away the minutes. We've got two days left in Padua.

Even H is dragging his tail around, and I do mean that literally. He is walking circles around the front room when I slink out of my bedroom for breakfast. My slipper scuffs on the wooden floor, sending him spinning around. His tail whacks into the coffee table, and the table leg makes an ominous crack.

Before I can stop him, he sucks in a breath and exhales a wave of flames over the broken furniture, turning it a crisp black. Then he wraps his arms around it and holds tight, bringing the object within his sphere long enough for the magic to fix the table leg back to new again.

Despite his heroic effort, Mathilde gripes at him from the kitchen table. "Be careful, H! This is a rental flat. We don't want to get stuck with a bill for damages."

"I didn't mean to do it, Tildy," he splutters. He casts a desperate glance my way, pleading for help.

There's no need for an intervention. Mathilde covers her face with her hands and huffs. She wipes her face and then apologises to our favourite wyvern. "Soz, H. I shouldn't have jumped on you. I know it was an accident. I don't know what's got into me."

"I do. The pressure of needing to solve this mystery is getting to all of us. I've been grumbling since I rolled out of bed." I pour myself a cup of coffee and join Mathilde at the table. The bruises under her eyes give the bags under mine a run for their money.

Unless we can change our attitudes and outlook, we don't stand a chance of solving this mystery. Staring at the wall for hours has rarely provided inspiration in the past. I decide then that we need to get out of our flat and do something different. Fortunately, I have a ready solution.

"Harry and I are due to tour more of the university buildings and the famous Scrovegni Chapel. Why don't you and Kate come along with us? I'm sure no one will mind. And who knows, maybe the fresh air and a walk through history will help us find a new angle to approach our mystery."

"I think that's a great idea," Harry says, appearing in the hallway. Unlike the rest of us, she's dressed for the day and her hair is perfectly combed into place.

"Why do you look so good?" I blurt. "I mean, compared to the rest of us. You have the most to lose."

Harry laughs at my blunt remark and gives us a knowing smile. "I believe in us, Nat. Time and again, we've faced terrifying opponents and odds not in our favour. And yet, we always come through in the end. So what that we don't have Oxford's magic and the collective knowledge of its Eternals to help us along? We've got each other. Anyone dumb enough to bet against us, or underestimate us, gets exactly what they deserve." She pats

Mathilde on the shoulder. "Chin up, Mathilde. We've got this. I promise."

Harry's impromptu pep talk works wonders on our mood. By the time Kate joins us, Harry has coaxed us into smiling and laughing. Our good humour is infectious, and before long, Kate agrees to our plan for the morning.

Outside, the air is cool, and the sky is overcast, reminding us of the problems lurking around us. Try as we might to put a smile on our faces, we can't completely abandon the thought that we're in a tight spot. Harry, however, is determined to keep our spirits up. As our group weaves through the warren of streets that make up Padua's centre, she draws us into conversation, asking about our partners back at home.

While we women are away, it seems the men have banded together and made the most of their few days of bachelorhood. I recount the story of Edward, Bartie, Trevor, and even my grandfather, meeting at my house for a poker night.

"I can't believe they played without me," H grumbles, spitting flames.

"I'm sure they'd be happy to do it again. If nothing else, it gives us women a good excuse to have one of our wine and cheese nights."

"Cheese night?" H rears back, his wings flapping madly. "Oi, missie! You four are 'aving cheese nights without me?"

"I, err, that is, um…" I stutter as my brain works furiously on finding a way out of the mess I've got myself into.

"Of course not," Kate replies, stepping into the gap. "We've talked about having one, but that's as far as we've got. Look, that gelateria looks like it's open. What do you say to a double-scoop of ice cream, H?"

As H swoops across the road to peek in the shop's front window, I pull out my purse and dash over to catch up. "I'll treat,

H. Consider it my way of saying sorry for hurting the feelings of my best mate."

One ice cream cone later, we arrive on time to find out our tour of the university is more of a tour of the university offices. It is as though every department head is keen to showcase their cabinet of awards and a litany of notable past faculty and students. While I want to tune out and let my mind work on the murder, I force myself to pay attention. After all, who knows how many of these historical personages are still running around as Eternals?

Even lunch offers no respite. We end up gathered around a dining hall table being peppered with questions about Oxford's tutorial system. I turn the matter over to Harry, as her knowledge is far beyond mine. Our only saving grace is that H isn't with us. After the first meeting, he begged me to let him go back to Caffé Pedrocchi to play with the giant stone lion statues.

Right as I lose all hope of making it out with my sanity intact, our host announces we need to run if we're going to make our appointment time at the Scrovegni Chapel. The walk over gives us all a much needed chance to stretch our legs. Even the lingering grey clouds obscuring the sun from view can't dampen our enthusiasm at being outdoors after a morning cooped inside.

Kate sidles up after we cross a street, practically thrumming with excitement. "You're going to be amazed by the frescoes. Nat. They are exceptional, especially when you consider how old they are."

"You've visited before? Wait, don't answer that. Of course you've been there before."

"When we were roommates, Lavinia told me all about them. The chapel is one of Padua's great prides. I made sure to visit when I came to her wedding."

From the outside, the reddish-pink bricks offer little hint of the masterpiece hidden inside its doors. It looks like a simple chapel, one of the thousands of them that occupies villages and town squares around the country.

Inside the chapel, however, is a different matter. Bright blue and brilliant golden highlights illuminate nearly every centimetre of the walls and ceiling. I hardly know where to look first, as each scene depicted in the frescoes is as captivating as the next. Our tour guide gives us a moment to take it all in before launching into an overview of the building's history and the stories depicted on the walls.

Despite the relatively small size of the chapel, we spend an hour exploring and gazing, letting the over seven-hundred-year-old paintings revive our spirits and lift our souls.

Before we leave, our guide invites us to circle up in the middle of the space. Keeping her voice low, she states, "Now that you've had time to take in the art, I'd like to take these last few minutes we have together to highlight a few of the aspects that make this chapel so incredible."

"Beyond the age of it?" Harry asks.

"Yes, although that is obviously of note. The first is Giotto's use of perspective to make the people he painted look three dimensional. Nowadays, we're accustomed to seeing things this way, but the technique didn't become popular until the Italian Renaissance more than one hundred years later. For early visitors it must have been shocking to see their icons depicted like real, rounded people rather than flat images."

"Second, note the way he weaves emotion into the journey, from a tender kiss between lovers to the tears on the faces of the mothers in the painting of the slaughter of the innocent."

We nod our understanding and the tour guide motions to another part of the space. "Giotto's aim was to depict the story of salvation, starting from when Mary discovered she was with child, through until Jesus rose from the dead and ascended into heaven. On the lower levels of the walls, he depicts the virtues and vices.

You can think of them as representing the duality of man. People may love or hate, be envious, or show great charity. We all make our choices as we go through our lives."

The guide chats for a few more minutes, but whatever she has left to say is lost on me. Without knowing it, the woman opened my eyes. Giotto's revolutionary approach to painting and storytelling has given me inspiration.

I tug Mathilde's sleeve, pulling her attention away from the frescoed walls. "Round up the others. I've got an idea for a new place to look for Angelina's murderer."

We hurry to say our goodbyes and thank our hosts and guide. I can tell from the looks on my friends' faces that they are eager to find out more about my revelation.

H is waiting in the gardens outside the chapel and comes flying over when he sees us leaving.

"Did you have fun with your new friends?" I ask.

"It was amazin', Nat! Remember the other day, 'ow they couldn't do more than swat me with their tails? Today, they could sit up and roar!"

"Roar?" My eyes grow wide as I imagine the chaos that caused.

"Don't lose your loaf, Nat. Nobody noticed," he reassures me. "It was just like back at 'ome. The magic made everyone ignore them."

H flies off to say hello to Mathilde, leaving me to ponder his explanation. My best guess is that somehow, the more time we spend here, the deeper our own connection to Padua grows. I shelve that thought, not wanting to distract myself from our biggest issue.

"Kate, can you see if Lavinia is available to meet us at her grandmother's house?"

"Sure thing, Nat," she replies. She types in a quick text and moments later, gets a reply. "She'll meet us there. We can grab a taxi on the main road. I've got the address."

The taxi driver is so delighted when a group of women slide into his taxi that he doesn't complain when H joins us. In broken English, he asks why we're in Padua and where we're from. Our attempts to answer in Italian have him roaring with laughter. We're all chuckling by the time we arrive at Nonna's front gate.

Lavinia takes one look at us and exclaims, "Please tell me you're this happy because you've got a new lead."

"It's too soon to say lead, but maybe a new avenue of investigation is the better way to put it," I reply. My answer intrigues everyone.

Inside the house, Lavinia's mum, grandmother, and Filippo are waiting on us. I'm thrilled to have both women and an experienced officer available to assist us. If I'm right about where we should look next, we'll need all the help we can get.

Despite Lavinia's desperation to know what I mean, Nonna refuses to take no for an answer when she offers coffee and tea.

"It's best if you say yes right away and let her get it over with," Lavinia advises us, before turning to her grandmother to add, "I'll help you in the kitchen, Nonna."

The rest of us head to the dining room. Before I take a seat, I stop to gather the photos and printouts we'd set aside for our chat with Signor Pavan. As Lavinia distributes cups of tea, I flip through the stack, refreshing my memory of their contents.

It takes two more trips to the kitchen, first for milk and sugar and then for a plate of biscotti, before Nonna gives us her blessing to start our discussion.

Without thinking about it, we've chosen the same seating arrangement as the evening before, only this time with Lavinia's mum in place of Signor Pavan. All eyes turn my way. I take a calming breath and then launch into an explanation of my new line of thought.

"Something the Chapel tour guide said made me rethink our logic. Although we started this investigation with a blank slate and an open mind, it didn't take us long to hone in on the idea that Angelina's death was somehow connected to her love life. We reduced the whole situation until it was black and white."

I shift until I focus on Filippo. "Early on, you said that if this case was a murder, you'd start by looking at Angelina's lovers, then family, and finally her friends. Last night, I was convinced we'd ticked all the boxes. Paolo was her secret love, Marco was her close friend, and we'd already figured out her family wasn't involved."

"There was never any doubt on that topic," Filippo adds in an aside to the three Italian women at the table.

"Today's talk got me thinking. Our tour guide explained Giotto had designed the lines of vices and virtues to be mirror images. Love can become hate under the right circumstances, and that was the path we followed. But there are other vices we should consider. Envy, pride, and anger can each drive someone to do the unthinkable."

I flip through the photos until I find the solo shot of Angelina laughing at something off camera. "We're missing someone else who was important to Angelina. Someone she trusted enough to let into her home, and maybe even to learn the truth of her secret relationship. We thought Signor Pavan took this photo, but he said someone else took it. Who was it?"

"Rosa." Nonna frowns, her brow wrinkling as she anticipates my next question.

"It can't be her," Lavinia's mum interjects. "She was Angelina's best friend, and had been for years. They were thick as thieves. Why would she do anything to hurt Angelina?"

I shrug. "I don't know, and I'm not saying it's her. But we have to at least consider the idea. If we can rule her out definitively, we'll widen the circle until we identify someone else."

Lavinia nods, adding her agreement. "Tell us about her, Nonna. You must have known her well."

"Not as well as you might think," she counters before growing silent. She drums her fingers on the table as she stares off into space, digging deep into the recesses of her memories for information on a woman she likely hasn't seen in years, maybe decades.

I risk a sip of my tea and am pleased to find it hasn't yet grown cold. H leaps onto the table, swipes a biscuit from the plate, and darts back under my chair before I can stop him. Not that I would... he has as much right to them as the rest of us.

His quick movements jar Nonna back to the present. She tuts at the daring cat, but lets the matter drop. Nonna motions towards Lavinia's mum. "Sandra is right. Angelina and Rosa were the best of friends and had been since they were children. Given our age difference, I dare say that Rosa was practically like a sister to her. When Angelina's husband died, it was Rosa who comforted her until she could stand on her own again."

"Did Rosa marry, or have a family of her own?"

"Yes, she was married, but she never had any children. The best I can describe it is to say she followed in Angelina's footsteps. If Angelina had given birth, I'm sure Rosa would have got pregnant as well. When my sister was left a widow, Rosa drifted away from her own husband. They stayed together, mind you, but they never struck me as particularly close or loving."

I glance at Filippo to see what he's making of this. He's leaned back in his chair, with his hands flat on the table and his head cocked to the side. Just like me, he is examining Nonna's words for anything which might hint at Rosa's guilt or innocence.

He digs deeper. "Did you notice any change in Rosa's behaviour either before or after Angelina's death?"

Nonna shakes her head. "I told you, I wasn't close to Rosa. I had my hands full with my children. Those two were unencumbered by that kind of baggage. Most evenings, they were off at some event. During the day, they worked in the same office. The Santo was one of the few places I saw them, and only when we stayed to help tidy the seating area after the service."

Filippo grimaces, his frustration over the lack of information clear for all of us to see.

I can't say the same. "The Santo? Do you mean the Basilica of Sant'Antonio?"

"Cosa?" Nonna asks, caught off guard. "Oh yes, in Padova we refer to it as the Santo."

The same Santo where Harry took a tumble off a staircase.

"Where did they work? Was it Palazzo Bo?"

"Sí, it was there." Nonna's eyes open wide. "But how did you know that?"

Before I can explain, Mathilde jumps in with a question of her own. "Where is Rosa buried?"

Nonna stares at us, unable to imagine where we are going with this line of questions, but answers despite her confusion. "She is buried near Angelina. One row over, if I'm not mistaken."

With those words, the final missing piece falls into place. I'm not sure what Rosa's motives were, but the circumstantial evidence is damning.

Lavinia thanks her mother and grandmother for their help and asks them for one last favour. "Mamma, would you mind picking up my bambine from school and keeping them at my house until Stefano gets home?"

"We'll both go," her mother replies, pointing between herself and Nonna. "Make sure to lock up after you leave." With that agreement in place, the old Italians depart.

"It has to be her," I half-whisper when I hear the front door close. Kate, who is closest to me, voices her agreement. Harry, Mathilde, and even H soon chime in.

"But why then?" Filippo asks. "The two women were so close. What would possess Rosa to kill her best friend in the world?"

"Maybe because Angelina was preparing to leave her," I propose. "In the metaphorical sense, not the literal one. Let's look at our evidence again. Angelina and Rosa were practically inseparable. With each passing year, the risk of Angelina getting married again, or going off to do her own thing, declined. And then Paolo Pavan comes onto the scene. He wants Angelina to marry him — to stay by his side and grow old together."

"Okay, I can see that," Filippo admits. "But then, why kill Angelina? Why not get rid of Paolo?"

I shrug. "Maybe she tried to get rid of him. Paolo said he did not know how his wife found out about his relationship with Angelina. Maybe Rosa told her. When that didn't work, she had to take it a step further."

Lavinia raises two fingers in the air. "Rage and jealousy, two powerful vices in their own right."

No one can deny the truth in her words.

Filippo, however, isn't done. He crosses his arms over his chest and levels his gaze on me. "You claim this ghost of Rosa is haunting Harry. What would be her motivation, especially if she's the one who killed Angelina?"

His tone is sharp, the challenge thrown out like a gauntlet. I suspect he's been waiting for this moment when he could finally prove to himself that all our talk of magic was nothing more than a figment of our imaginations.

Unlucky for him, I'm not one to back down. I take my time to reason through everything we know and suspect. In the end, the answer is as obvious as the nose on my face.

"Rosa's deepest fear was being separated from Angelina. Death should have been the ultimate bond. Seeing Harry walking through the hallways of Palazzo Bo would have absolutely enraged her. She wouldn't have seen a British woman with a remarkable resemblance to her old friend."

"She saw me with Lavinia," Harry says. "I became Angelina, rejoined with her family, and once again out of her reach."

Filippo frowns but stays quiet. Deep inside, he knows he's been defeated. There's no need to rub it in his face. He's served his purpose and helped us solve a fifty-year-old crime. Whether he believes in the existence of the Eternals is irrelevant.

Now, we've got more important things to worry about. Namely, how do we confirm our suspicions and put a stop to Rosa before she can strike again?

I straighten in my chair and hunt around for my handbag, but H has beaten me to the punch. He pokes me in the leg with his talon to get my attention.

"Lookin' for this?" He waves my notebook and pen in the air. "Get a move on it, Nat. We've got limited time and lots of plannin' to do iffen we're gonna get justice for Angelina before it's time to go 'ome."

Chapter Fifteen

Of course, planning a trap isn't as easy as scribbling a few notes in my book. Lavinia suggests we decamp to the more comfortable chairs in the front room.

We invite Filippo to join us. For a moment, he wavers, and I almost think his desire to see things through to the end will be enough to overpower his doubts. However, his inner skeptic rears its head, and he declines, citing work obligations.

We're all disappointed with his decision to turn his back on the case before its conclusion, but what can we do?

Lavinia's shoulders hunch as we watch him walk out the front gate. I throw an arm over her and give her a quick squeeze of support. "Don't worry too much about Filippo, okay? These things have a way of working themselves out."

"Really?" She exhales while looking skyward, almost as though she is sending out a request for the universe to help.

I can remember feeling the same way after Trevor, Mathilde's boyfriend, reacted badly to the news that magic was real. It had all come out okay in the end, and I had to believe this time would be no different.

"Give him some time," I suggest. "We've got plenty to keep us busy for the next twenty-four hours. Worst-case scenario, you can talk to him again after we're gone. Maybe some time for reflection will help open his mind to things he can't imagine."

Back inside, we get comfortable in the front room. H stretches out on the windowsill, keeping guard. Kate and Harry take either end of the sofa, leaving the middle seat for Lavinia. Mathilde curls up in the armchair, wrapping her arms around her legs as much for comfort as warmth. As for me, I take my normal position at the front of the room. As always, I'm armed with pen, paper, and plenty of ideas.

"Alright team, we've got a pretty good idea who is responsible for Angelina's death and the attacks on Harry. The question we've got to tackle now is how to stop her. Anyone want to start us off?"

I survey the room and smile when Mathilde waves her hand. "Excellent. What's on your mind, Mathilde?"

"We've held off making a proper connection between Padua and the Earth's magical field. Now, I think it is time we take the next step. We're going to have to communicate with Rosa - either to rule her out or to get her to confess. When we wanted to speak with Angelina, we picked a place we thought would resonate with her. I suggest we do the same here."

"Good thinking!" I jot some notes on the page. "We've had encounters in three locations — Palazzo Bo, Saint Anthony's Basilica, and the cemetery."

"I wouldn't suggest Palazzo Bo," Harry pipes up. "The building is huge, with multiple floors and tons of offices and rooms. Not to mention the daily visitors and people who work there."

"We've got the same problem with the Santo," Lavinia agrees. "It's a pilgrimage destination and is always crawling with people. I wouldn't want to do anything which risks damaging the cathedral."

I glance at the remaining location and can't hold back a

grimace. "Ugh. Not the cemetery again. Who knows what other Eternals are lurking out of sight on its grounds? And if we end up having to make a run for it, I do not want to have to hurdle tombstones to get to safety." I tap my pen against my chin, willing my mind to come up with another solution.

"What if we approach this question from a different angle?" Kate suggests. "Instead of thinking of the places where Rosa would be strongest, let's think about what location would best serve our needs. Why shouldn't we have the advantage for once?"

I flip over to a clean page and make a new list, immediately latching onto Kate's proposal. "First, I'd prefer to be out in the open, and nowhere near any wooden balconies or flying office supplies."

Harry snorts at my comment and gives me a thumb's up.

"Second, I'd lean toward a location that gives us the best chance of success in establishing a connection with the magical field."

"What do you need for that?" Lavinia asks.

Mathilde answers, having memorised the information. "According to the instructions we received from the men who discovered the magic of Oxford, we need a location with a long, meaningful history that is still significant today. Wherever that is, it must have space for us to build a circle to anchor the connection."

Lavinia stares out the window, deep in thought. "There are several piazzas in the centre of town that would fit that criteria. They're all fairly close together. How do we narrow it down?"

That's the critical question, and none of us have an answer. If we'd succeeded even once before now, perhaps we'd feel confident to take a gamble. But we haven't.

Despite his intense watch out the window, H is obviously listening to our discussions. He launches into the air and flies to a new position on top of the wooden desk.

"Oi, Livvy! What's the name of the oval park with the giant fountain in the middle of it? The one with all the statues."

Lavinia thinks for a second. "Prato della Valle?"

"That's the one!" H rasps. "What about it?"

"It would be perfect. I can't believe I didn't think of it first." Lavinia leans forward, her hands waving in excitement. "It is practically a circle, so that meets one requirement. It's hundreds of years old, but also a point of pride for us Padovani since it is the largest square in Italy. More importantly, it's only a few minutes' walk from the Santo. If we can come up with a way to lure Rosa there, it would be our best option by far."

I try to picture what the Prato looks like, but we've seen so many places since we arrived that it has become a blur. Fortunately, one quick search on the internet later, and I've got a bird's-eye view right on my phone. I pass it around the room so my friends can see as well.

Prato della Valle is closer to an oval than a square. Even though prato translates as lawn in English, there isn't any grass in sight. Instead, it is a concrete walkway lined with statues representing Padua's best and brightest. A narrow canal circles the oval, with four footpaths providing access to cross it.

"We've got the special copper rods Sir Christopher Wren designed," I murmur. "Normally, we'd rely on sunlight, but what if we dropped them into the water that encircles the inner ring? If we direct enough light onto the water, it would not only glow, but it would also form a natural connection between the rods." I point to the image. "We could drop one off the side of each of the four footbridges."

"It might work," Mathilde says. "I'd want to run the idea past the Eternals in Oxford. Could Edward help me arrange a call with your grandfather?"

"I'm sure he'd be happy to do it. We should phone him now, since he and Trevor are supposed to fly down tomorrow to join us for the Twinning Ceremony." I flip through my phone screens until I find Edward's number. When the call starts to ring, I pass the phone to Mathilde and leave the conversation with her. She steps into the hallway, finding a quiet space to handle her assignment.

H and Harry are chatting quietly while looking at a photo on Harry's phone. When Harry sees I'm free, she waves me over. "Prato della Valle is gigantic, Nat. Even if we manage to connect to the magic and trap Rosa within the inner circle, there is still a lot of ground to cover. We need backup."

I zoom in on the photo, taking a closer look at the layout. It takes a few more clicks and a couple of internet searches before I land on a solution. "I've got some ideas of where we can get some support, but I'll need Lavinia and H to help."

The pair are more than willing to do whatever is needed and agree without asking for an explanation. I update my notepad with the new assignments. As I skim the list, I can't help but laugh.

"What's so funny?" Kate asks.

"You can take the prefects out of Oxford, but you can't keep us from living up to our calling. We've got Mathilde on research, you're gathering supplies and artefacts, and I'm responsible for making sure all the right people show up."

"If we were looking for a sign that we're on the track, we couldn't ask for anything clearer than that," Kate agrees.

Harry rolls her eyes at us and motions for me to pass her my notepad. She reads through my notes and then raises her head to catch my attention. "You forgot one thing, Nat. I'm assuming we want to do this after dark. Where are we going to get a big, bright light to shine on the water?"

"We're going to use a torch," I reply, nodding at the wyvern sitting beside her. "A very, very large, magical torch."

❖

The next morning, we gather after breakfast to coordinate our plans for the day. Kate and Harry's assignment has me nervous.

"We'll be fine," Harry reassures me. "Kate and I will have a quick whip around the Santo, just long enough to drop a few hints about my plan to return later."

"I'll make sure she avoids any stairs and doesn't stray close to any moveable displays," Kate adds in a reassuring tone. "Then we'll stop for a coffee to refuel before tackling our next task. We will finish by noon so you two can make your final twinning ceremony meetings with the university team."

A dozen additional warnings cross my mind, but I bite my tongue and let them go. Kate and Harry are both adults, and neither will appreciate me mothering them, no matter how good my intentions are.

After they leave, Mathilde disappears into her bedroom with her laptop and a mug of tea. She's thrilled at the prospect of spending the morning searching the Bodleian Library archives. Although I somewhat envy her ability to spend the morning indoors, there's no way I'd swap places with her. While Mathilde loves curling up with a history book, I'd much prefer to chat with the Eternals who witnessed the events firsthand.

Outside, the morning air is warmer than it seemed from the overcast sky. The forecast promises the haze will burn off, leaving it sunny later in the day. Lavinia is quiet as we begin our walk to Palazzo Bo. The second time I catch her smoothing her shirt, I ask whether she is okay.

"I'm cosí cosí," she answers in Italian, wobbling her hand from side to side as an explanation. "Not about this evening, but about what we're doing now. I'm a little nervous."

"About meeting another Eternal?"

"Not just any Eternal," she corrects me. "Elena Cornaro! Do

you have any idea how many times I've walked past her statue at Palazzo Bo? You'd be hard pressed to find a woman in Padova who isn't at least somewhat familiar with her name. In a city full of statues of men, she certainly stands out."

"From what little I could speak with her before, I can assure you she is warm and friendly. I suspect you will find her to be one of your top supporters once we get the current situation behind us."

Lavinia halts in her tracks. "Nat, I haven't even thought that far ahead yet!"

"Does it make things better or worse?" I ask, chuckling.

"Better," she assures me. "Knowing I'll have more chances to get to know her takes some of the pressure off the first meeting. Thanks for the reminder."

My answering smile quickly turns into laughter when H spins around from ahead of us, shouting for us to shake a leg. "You're not the only one who's in a hurry."

By now I've learned the way from our flat to the historic university building. We skip the main entrance, instead choosing the secondary arched doorway closer to the historic courtyard where Elena's statue is located. The courtyard is quiet, with only a few people milling around. None pay us any mind as we stroll toward the statue sitting in the stairwell.

Lavinia stops on the stairs and looks over her shoulder at where I'm coming up behind her. "How does this work, Nat?"

"Last time, we were able to speak with her very briefly when H was in contact with the marble statue. I wanted you to come along, because I hoped your presence would strengthen the connection." I step aside and let H get in front of us. "H, do you mind sitting in her lap again? And Lavinia, maybe you can touch the hand she has outstretched."

The pair do as I suggest, but nothing happens. I tilt my head to the side, studying the scene, when it hits me what we're missing. "H, your fire. Can you warm her up?"

H sucks in a deep breath and then sends a wave of reddish orange flames flowing over the statue's head, taking care to avoid getting too close to Lavinia. As soon as the flames clear, the statue blinks into awareness, and her mouth curves into a warm smile.

"Hello again," she says, laughing as H rubs his head against her chin. He curls in her lap and purrs in contentment.

Lavinia gasps when Elena Cornaro shifts her marble hand and twines their fingers together. Just as I'd hoped, the combination of H's magic and Lavinia's connection to Padua allow Elena to speak and move with ease.

"Elena, meet Lavinia, Padua's first magical prefect. Lavinia, meet Elena Cornaro Piscopia, Padua's first Eternal."

Lavinia bows her head in a formal greeting, too awestruck to put her excitement into words. Elena glances down at their linked hands, marvelling as well.

"I can see so clearly and even move my hands. I never imagined having so much freedom," Elena says.

"If all goes to plan, you'll be able to do much more than that," Lavinia tells her.

Seeing the women react to one another makes me wish we could linger for as long as we want. Based on my own experiences, I know how strong the bond is between prefects and Eternals.

But today, however, we have a mission, and limited time to accomplish it. After giving the women a moment, I clear my throat and call their attention my way. "Elena, we need your help to solve a crime that spans from the past into the present. An Eternal is attacking innocent women, and we must put a stop to it."

"An Eternal?" Elena rears back in shock. "How could an Eternal hurt one of the living?"

Lavinia keeps the explanation as concise as possible. Elena's expression grows more and more grave. By the time Lavinia finishes, Elena appears on the verge of spitting fire.

"I will help you in any way that I can," she assures us. "Tell me what you need."

This time I take the lead, taking Elena through the plan we assembled the night before. "If all goes well, Harry and I will lure Rosa from the Santo to Prato della Valle. Once there, we'll spring our trap. Our first aim is to wring a confession from her, or at a minimum, get her to reveal information that will confirm our suspicions. After that, it will be left to Eternals such as yourself to see her punished for her actions."

"You choice of location will make my task easier," Elena replies. "I will find your Zia Angelina and rally our troops."

Lavinia tears up as she thanks Elena for her immediate willingness to come to our aid. Elena gives her hand one last squeeze and then sends us on our way.

Lavinia unclasps their hands and steps back. Elena manages a small wave of goodbye before H flaps his wings and lifts until he can look me in the eye.

"It worked, Nat! That's the longest conversation we've ever managed. And did you see 'ow much she could move?"

"Let's hope the same holds true for your lion friends," I say. "But you're right to celebrate this accomplishment. This little experiment gives me great hope for our chances of success — both in capturing Rosa and in creating a stable connection between Padua and the magical field."

It's a short walk to Caffè Pedrocchi. The four stone lions are in exactly the same position as before, basking in the sunlight which is peeking through the clouds. They are at once both majestic and fearsome. We couldn't possibly find better allies to face off against an evil Eternal.

The question, however, is how do we get them from their

home in the middle of the historic centre to Prato della Valle, a fifteen-minute walk away?

H takes one look at the smattering of patrons sitting on the terrace and points to the furthest lion from them. "Let's start with Leo over there," he suggests.

"They have names?" I blurt, caught off guard.

H snorts a smokey laugh in response to my expression. "Iffen they do, they 'aven't shared them with me. I've been calling them all Leo. It's short for leone, the Italian word for lion."

H soars over the plaza and lands with a thump on Leo's back. He barely has a second to catch his balance before the stone lion yawns and sits up. Just as H had said, none of the passersby note the statue's movements. They wander past, continuing along their way without a clue about the magic taking place in their midst.

"Do you know how many times I imagined riding on these lions?" Lavinia asks. "I was forever running off from my mamma and papá so I could scrabble onto their backs and pretend they were alive."

"How does seeing the real thing compare to your childhood imagination?"

"Oh Nat, it's even better. This is truly the most wonderful gift you, Kate, and Mathilde have given me. I don't think I will ever stop being amazed at what the magic can bring to life."

I'm smiling so widely I can feel my eyes crinkling at their corners. "We feel exactly the same way, Lavinia. No other job could ever compare to that of being a prefect."

H waves us over and makes the introductions.

Lavinia outstretches her hand, but stops herself at the last moment. "Do you think... I mean, that is... can I touch him?"

The lion answers by shifting his head until he can snuffle her fingers. She giggles in utter delight, and dares to run her fingers through this mane. The stone waves and shifts just like real hair.

The lion rumbles in pleasure as Lavinia strokes his head and scratches behind his ears. All the while, she's telling him our plans and what help is needed.

"Can you help us? Is the magic strong enough to permit you to leave your place here on the steps of the Pedrocchi?"

The lion lifts his head and stares at the sky. I can hardly breathe as my heart pounds with nerves. The beast shifts his head again, turning until he can see the wyvern perched on his back. Then he speaks. Or roars, I should say. His answer is incomprehensible to me, but H seems to have no trouble understanding.

H slides off the lion's back and lands at his flank, moving backwards until their tails are twisted together. Under our gaze, the lion shivers and shakes, sending trickles of fine sand into the air. The stone groans and creaks until a pair of wings emerge from below the surface.

"Il leone di San Marco!" Lavinia exclaims, the first of us to make sense of the change. "It is the symbol of power for the Veneto, Nat."

The winged lion whips his tail into the air and launches H onto his back. With two mighty pumps of his wings, the pair takes flight. I stand, my mouth agape, as they circle the piazza, casting an impossible lion-shaped shadow onto the concrete.

Then, they land, and the lion sinks back into its original position, the wings disappearing from sight. Even after a year of interacting with magical creatures and Eternal spirits, I am still shocked into silence.

H is not. He whoops with joy and calls for us to follow him to the next lion. One by one, H and Lavinia visit each of the four lions. By working together, they're able to empower the lions. Lavinia's connection to the beasts remains, even after she ceases to be in direct contact. As long as H is there to share his own magical field, the lions can fly.

I send a quick text to our friends to let them know we'll have enough Eternals to guard the Prato and prevent Rosa from escaping. I turn to leave, but Lavinia doesn't follow. She's still staring at the lions, lost in thought.

"Something wrong?" I ask, wondering what we've overlooked.

Lavinia turns to me, her mouth pinched tight. "You know, Nat, I'd already decided Filippo was a fool for refusing to believe that magic is real. But only now am I grasping just how much he is going to miss. Talking with the most famous scholars from history, soaring the skies atop the lion of San Marco... he would revel in these experiences."

She's absolutely right, but there's not much else I can say. "Being a prefect is a calling, Lavinia. If he can't hear the call, someone else will take his place. All we can do is wait and see."

"Not wait and see," she corrects me, her face hardening in determination. "We will act, Nat. Together, we'll do whatever it takes to allow Padova's magic to flourish."

Chapter Sixteen

A shiver runs down my spine as I stand in the darkness. It is nearing midnight and we're putting our final preparations into place in Prato della Valle. For the last half hour, the oval plaza has been a hive of activity. All around me are familiar faces. I walk over to the closest person, a tall man with wavy brown hair and sky-blue eyes. He pulls me into a hug, resting his chin on the top of my head, and I sigh with happiness.

"I'm so glad you and Trevor made it in time to be here tonight. We women could have done this on our own, but having you two standing with us makes me feel better."

"There's no place I'd rather be than at your side, Nat," Edward replies.

I tilt my head back so I can look him in the face. "Even if I'm facing off against an evil Eternal in a murderous rage?"

"Especially then!" He shakes his head as the unreality of our conversation hits us both. "Life with you will never be boring."

I don't offer a defence, especially since my wyvern is circling over our heads, riding bareback on a winged stone lion. The lion lands with surprising grace and trots over to sit with the three lions who proceeded him. The four sit like points on a compass around the central fountain, guarding the entire plaza.

A splash grabs my attention. Mathilde and Trevor are leaning over the footbridge, watching as one of our magical copper rods sinks to the bottom of the man-made canal which separates the outer oval from the inner one. Kate does the same from the other side of the park and Lavinia quickly follows suit from her position on the third footbridge. Edward reaches into his pocket and produces the last gleaming rod. He gives me a quick kiss and whispers words of good luck before marching to the remaining bridge.

I search the area until I spot a white-haired woman dressed in loose-fitting trousers and running shoes. She waves and then points at her watch, reminding me it is time for us to go. All I can do is trust in the power of the magic and hope our plans are enough to see us through this final challenge.

Harry and I stay close together as we walk along the silent street toward the Basilica of Saint Anthony. The brief journey gives us time to mentally review our next moves and to gather our courage for what we must do next. Our plan hinges on Rosa taking the bait. Harry and I have to dangle it in front of her.

We stop across the street from the enormous church. Old-fashioned street lamps line the edge of the church grounds. Their golden circles of light fight valiantly against the darkness, but it is a losing battle. There are too few of them to win out over the shadows.

Adrenaline hums through my body. I shake my hands at my side, urging myself to be calm. If Harry is suffering from the same stress, she shows no sign of it. With her hands on her hips, she gazes across the street without showing an ounce of fear.

"I know Rosa thinks you're Angelina, but taking it a step further might put you in even more danger. Are you sure you're ready to play this role?

She takes a deep, cleansing breath before she answers me. "You're darn right, I am. I've had enough of running scared. It's time we turned the tables." Without a sideways glance, Harry squares her shoulders and strides toward the towering arches that line the front of the church.

I rush to catch-up and am grateful there are no cars or people to block my way. As soon as my feet hit the paved courtyard, I launch into the first lines of our scripted conversation.

"Angelina, wait!" I shout, my voice hoarse with nerves.

Harry spins around to face me. "Don't try to talk me out of it. Paolo and I are in love. He's asked me to marry him and I plan to say yes."

"But you can't leave me," I argue, grabbing onto Harry's arm. "We go everywhere together. Paolo will be in the way."

"Aren't you listening, Rosa? I said I love him. Can't you see how happy he makes me? Don't I deserve to find someone after all these years alone?" Harry pulls her arm from my grasp just as a strong wind whips my hair into my face.

The sky overhead is clear and the night still and quiet. The wind can't be natural. It can only mean one thing.

"It's her," I whisper between gritted teeth.

Harry's eyes widen in fear, but she doesn't back down. We'd planned a longer conversation in case it was needed. Harry skips to the end, not wanting to hang around here any longer than necessary.

"Don't make me choose between him and you, Rosa," Harry growls. "You won't like how the story ends."

"I won't let you leave me behind," I argue, closing my hands into fists.

Harry takes a deep breath and repositions herself so she is facing the direction of Prato della Valle. She gathers her energy and throws down her last words. "Then you'll have to catch me!"

Harry takes off running. She's in great shape and I have trouble keeping up as she dashes up the empty pavement.

The wind picks up pace, shoving me from behind. Rosa wants me to catch her friend. She's determined to see me win.

The lid of a nearby bin hits the ground with a clatter. Rubbish flies into the air, taking a vaguely humanoid shape.

"Run, Harry!" I shout as I dig into my reserves and push my body to the limit. Every second passes in slow motion as aluminium soda cans and wads of paper swirl in the air.

My vision narrows until all I can see is the wide open space growing larger with every step. When I see H sitting atop an empty pedestal, I nearly cry with relief. We're so close. All we need to do is get across the footbridge.

That's when Harry stumbles. Her rhythmic steps go off beat as she lurches sideways. Her shriek pierces the air. Lightning shoots across my nerves and I pick up speed, running faster than I ever have before.

I hold out an arm and catch Harry before she can fall and hurt herself. Terror propels us those last few steps until we bound across the concrete bridge.

I look back in time to see H assume his true size, ballooning from a cat-sized wyvern into a fire-breathing monster many times my height. He opens his mouth and sends a jet of magical flames licking across the surface of the canal.

Just as we'd hoped, the waters carry the flames, making the entire canal glow in vivid shades of gold and crimson.

The air is electrified as the connection to the magical field struggles to take hold. The rest of our group rush to join us, with Edward, Trevor and Mathilde on my right and Kate and Lavinia on Harry's left. We link arms, forming a human wall of protection. If Rosa wants a fight, she'll have to take all of us.

Around us, Eternals flicker into view, filling the inner oval. There are dozens of them, dressed in old-fashioned clothing and holding weapons of all shapes and sizes. The four lions wind between them, marking their prey.

However, it is the two women facing off at the base of the footbridge who hold our attention. The first I recognise as Lavinia's Zia Angelina. Her resemblance to Harry is remarkable, despite longer hair and clothing from the 1970s. Across from her can only be Rosa. In the shimmering orange firelight, her face is half-shadowed. But, there is enough visible for me to match her features with a woman we'd seen in Angelina's old photos.

Rosa throws herself at Angelina, and the pair disappears from view.

All the Eternals vanish and the lions freeze in place, once again stone.

"The magic, H!" I cry. "The connection isn't strong enough. We need more fire!"

H obliges, roaring again to set the water ablaze. When the first sparks hit the canal, the magic strengthens again enough for us to see the Eternals. Angelina has her arms wrapped around Rosa, struggling to hold her back. Rosa only has eyes for Harry, and her gaze is murderous.

In a moment of absolute clarity, I realise we've made a huge mistake. Despite all our efforts and planning, magic alone won't be enough. My breathing goes ragged as panic closes my throat.

Our taunts have infuriated an enraged Eternal, hellbent on wiping Angelina's existence from the Earth.

And I can't see any way to stop her.

Pounding footsteps jerk me back to the present. I lean forward and look to my left, wondering who it might be. A woman with long, blonde hair sprints over a footbridge. When her feet land in the inner oval, the Eternals regain their visibility.

Although the woman is a stranger, she isn't alone. Elena Cornaro Piscopia stands with her, resting her hand on the woman's back.

I stare, unable to make sense of it. Why would Elena bring another human to join our fight?

"It's our guide," Harry gasps in recognition. "The woman who showed us around Scrovegni Chapel!"

"She's meant to be a prefect!" Mathilde adds. "She must be. Why else would Elena bring her here?"

Elena Cornaro whispers instructions, guiding the woman until she joins our group. On instinct, Lavinia holds out a hand. The woman accepts the gesture and completes the link.

The canal glows brighter and the Eternals gain strength. But they continue to waver in and out of view. Rosa is still fighting to be free, while Angelina barely hangs on.

We're still missing something. Someone.

"Come on," I mumble, twisting my head left and right as I search for any sign of one last arrival. "We're counting on you. You have to show up!"

A man's shout ripples across the open space, echoing off the hard ground and surrounding buildings.

"Ferma!" he yells.

I know that voice. So does Lavinia.

"Filippo!" she cries in relief as he steps onto the bridge behind Angelina and Rosa.

His appearance is the missing link. An intangible feeling ripples across the air, making my ears pop and my eyes water.

Filippo, ever the police officer, only has eyes for the two women fighting in front of him. He strides over to them and rips them apart, shoving Angelina aside as he grabs firmly onto Rosa.

"What is the meaning of this?" he shouts at Lavinia and the rest of us. Only then does he notice the other people standing in the Prato. All around him, Eternal ghosts and magical creatures stare back at him.

I want to say that it's magic, but the words fail to materialise. I'm too wired with nerves to string together anything coherent.

Fortunately, there is someone else on hand who can offer an explanation.

A kind-faced man with a bushy white beard steps out from the group of Eternals. In his black velvet doublet and tights, he predates our time by centuries.

Filippo's eyes widen and his eyebrows shoot skyward. His mouth moves, but no words come out. He splutters a cough and swallows to wet his throat. Then we can hear him.

"Non è possibile!" he argues with himself. "It cannot be him. It is an actor. A fake."

The Eternal doesn't stop until he is standing directly in front of Filippo, looking him in the eye. He reaches out and takes Rosa from Filippo's grasp. With the fight now drained out of her, he has no trouble tossing her to a nearby lion.

Rosa lands at the feet of the creature. The winged lion settles a massive paw on her back, holding her in place with ease.

"You know who I am, Filippo. Say my name," the ancient Eternal orders with a grave expression.

"Gali... Galileo?" Filippo can barely get the word out.

Everyone in our group rocks backwards, stunned at having this famous astronomer in our midst.

Galileo gives a single nod of confirmation. "Touch my hand, if you must. I am here, and as solid as you are, Filippo."

Filippo's hand shakes as he gently pats Galileo's shoulder and arm.

"Filippo, you are called to be a praefectus of Padova. I know you are wary to believe what your eyes and hands tell you is real, but you must listen to me." Galileo shifts position, half-turning so he can address our group and Filippo. "I know better than most how shocking it is to discover that a truth you hold dear is wrong. This is the position in which you now find yourself. There exists a realm for spirits, one which encircles the Earth. The Oxford prefects have managed the impossible — they have helped you forge a connection between your realm and mine. They call it magic. I prefer to call it science."

Filippo shakes his head, still not ready to take that irrevocable step of acceptance. "This is a dream..."

"It is no dream," Galileo corrects him, growing frustrated with Filippo's pigheadedness. "You think you can invent something this elaborate? What of your friend Lavinia? What reason would she have to mislead you? Only wilful ignorance can explain continued resistance, Filippo. I've watched you study in our university lecture rooms. You are smarter than this."

Filippo flinches as the figurative blow lands.

"You must be brave, Filippo," Galileo says, his tone deep and powerful. "Brave explorers are the only men and women capable of pushing knowledge and invention forward. When evidence speaks louder than deeply held beliefs, you must have the courage to admit you are wrong and accept a new truth. Tell me, Filippo. Can you do this? Are you strong enough to set aside what you know and step into the unknown?"

Filippo stands still for so long that I fear he will say no. Gradually, his shoulders loosen and calm smooths his expression. He takes a long look at everyone around him — our Oxford group, Lavinia and the strange woman, and the dozens of Eternals in various forms of dress. He breathes deeply, his chest expanding, and bestows on us a beatific smile.

"I will do it. I will become a prefect."

Lavinia gives a half-sob, half-cheer and runs over to envelop her brother-in-law in a hug.

But the Eternals aren't done. Elena Cornaro claps her hands to draw our attention.

"There are still two more who must accept our call. Lavinia and Chiara," she pauses, motioning for the two Italian women to join her. Lavinia and the tour guide walk to stand before her. "We need at least three prefects to stabilise our connection. Filippo will represent the people of Padova. Lavinia, you would work on behalf of art and creativity. And Chiara, you will represent knowledge and progress. Are you two willing to do this? I warn you, it is not a calling you will find easy to relinquish."

Lavinia says yes with no hesitation. Chiara, the tour guide, takes a moment longer.

"What happens if I agree? Will I be able to see you? To see all of this?" she asks.

"All this and so much more," Elena promises. "Together, the three of you will create a connection which encompasses the entire city, and will stand to benefit this generation and all the ones to come."

"Then my answer is a resounding *sí*," Chiara agrees. "Yes, and yes again."

Everyone bursts into spontaneous applause to celebrate the momentous occasion. When it dies down, I'm pulled into a warm embrace. Harry hugs me and whispers in my ear how proud she is of us. She pulls back long enough for Kate and Mathilde to join us. "I had full faith that the three of you would forge a new magical connection. All you needed were the missing ingredients and the right inspiration."

"Inspiration?" I blurt, unable to halt a laugh. "More like desperation. When it comes to keeping you safe, Harry, even the impossible can't stand in our way."

"We've got one matter left to settle," Filippo shouts. We turn to see him standing over Rosa, who is still trapped by the lion.

Angelina joins him, looking down at her past friend with a sorrowful gaze. "Rosa, why did you do this? You were my best friend, and yet you murdered me and haunted these other women who share my resemblance."

"You were going to move on, Angelina. I could see the way

you looked at Paolo when you thought no one was watching. You were going to leave me behind, and I couldn't stand it."

"Oh Rosa," Angelina sobs, choking back her tears. "How I felt about Paolo, and whatever my intentions were in his regard, was irrelevant. You had always been there for me, in my worst times and in my best. How could you think I could ever replace you?"

"You already had," Rosa replies, her tone growing cold as ice. "You spurned my offers to go away so you could spend time with him. It was one step, but the first of many, no doubt."

Filippo glances between the two women, knowing he has to take action, but unsure what to do. He can hardly drag a ghost to jail.

"Leave Rosa with us," Galileo offers. "Antenor, you were a wise counsellor. Will you see she is properly punished?"

A man strides out from the group, his muscular form draped in classical Greek clothing. He leans over and takes Rosa by the wrist and the pair blinks from sight.

Angelina thanks us all for our help in seeing Rosa stopped, and justice served. "I feel I owe a particular thanks to you, Harry, for stepping into my shoes and facing off against my enemy. A lesser woman would have turned tail and run."

Harry blushes as she brushes off Angelina's thanks, far too British to allow for any greater display of emotion outside of her closest friends.

With all matters resolved, the group breaks off into clusters. Edward sticks at my side as I make a beeline for H. Once again in his small size, he basks in the flurry of compliments I rain over him. Without his help, we'd never have created the initial magical connection.

By the time we're done, I notice Bartie has also appeared and is standing at Kate's side as she introduces him to her friend Lavinia. I can only imagine how special that moment must feel for both Kate and Bartie. They've had so few chances to share news of the relationship with the important people in their lives.

Although I'd like nothing more than to spend hours speaking with Padua's Eternals and meeting the newest prefects, the late hour weighs on all of us. When I can no longer hold back the yawns, I suggest we call it a night and regroup in the morning.

One by one, the Eternals take their leave, returning to their normal posts. In the blink of an eye, they travel from the middle of Prato della Valle, back to their positions on the column pedestals that line the canal.

When there is no one left but our group of friends, old and new, I take a moment to check that everything is as it should be. Near the end of a nearby footbridge, a pedestal is empty.

"Are we missing someone?" I ask to no one in particular.

Chiara, the newest prefect, is the one to respond. "No, that one has been empty for as long as I can remember." She stares at the vacant space, her brow scrunched up in thought. "Maybe it is time for someone else to join the ranks of our exalted citizens… perhaps a female, for a change."

"I know just the right Eternal for the job," I reply. The city of Padua may not know it, but it certainly owes Elena Cornaro Piscopia its thanks.

Chapter Seventeen

We get a late start the next morning, as all of us needed the extra rest after staying out until the wee hours. With Edward, Trevor, and Bartie joining us in the rental flat, we're practically bursting at the seams. After a hasty discussion, we decide to go out for breakfast.

We file out of the building and onto the city centre street. Mathilde takes the lead, with Trevor at her side. I'm amazed to see Padua's inhabitants going about their daily life. None of them have a clue about the momentous events of the evening before. To them, our group looks like any other bunch of tourists out for a day of sightseeing.

That thought leads to a stark realisation. Despite having spent a week in Padua, I've barely seen anything. All my plans to wander through the Italian designer shops and maybe even splurge on a new pair of shoes went right out the window. I cheer myself up by promising I can come back for another visit anytime I want. Now that I've got a local connection, there's no excuse not to pop in from time to time.

If H is disappointed that our plans were turned upside down, he doesn't show it. He flies beside Edward, already licking his snout at the thought of a cream-filled croissant and a cup of steamed milk. "Wait till you see 'ow many pastries they 'ave, mate. There's cream-filled, chocolate-filled, jam-filled…"

Harry and I have to bite our lips to keep from laughing at H's never-ending enthusiasm for food.

"I'll stick with a single croissant, but I need at least two cappuccinos," I confess. "If we didn't have so much to do before the twinning ceremony, I'd have happily slept for another hour."

"You're not the only one. I'm too old to be sprinting up and down streets at midnight."

"Oh, please!" I wave off her comment. "Harriet Dalrymple, you run circles around us all on a regular basis. Don't even bother trying to claim that one little mad dash wore you out. I refuse to believe it."

"She's right," Kate chimes in from behind us. "You're super human, Harry. We all know it."

I slide closer to Harry, making space for Kate to walk beside us. "I'm sorry Bartie couldn't come with us."

"That's okay," she assures me. "He's off coordinating with Padua's Eternals on a list of places we should bring into the magical border."

"Are you still planning to extend it to cover Palazzo del Bo today? It would be lovely if Bartie could join us for the formal ceremony."

"It's at the top of our list. While you and Harry are rubbing shoulders with the city and university leaders, the rest of us will toil away at distributing the copper rods around the city."

"In that case, you'll need plenty of energy. I'd better treat you all to breakfast."

The rest of the morning flies by, just as Kate predicted. Harry and I keep busy with discussions of seating arrangements and the order of speakers, among other endless tasks which should have been settled long earlier.

Finally, the rest of the Oxford delegation arrives. Dr Radcliffe gives us a warm greeting as soon as she sees us waiting outside Palazzo del Bo. She quickly introduces me to the few people I haven't met. I'm surprised to learn our own Professor Abate is from Padua and make a note to ask Lavinia if she's ever met him.

Shortly before two in the afternoon, I hear someone calling my name. Mathilde waves as she, Kate, Edward, Trevor, and even Bartie stride into the formal event hall where the ceremony will take place.

"This place is incredible," she gushes, her eyes feasting on the frescoed ceiling.

"It's called the Aula Magna for a reason," I remind her. "Although it is translated as the Great Hall in English, magnificent is how I'd describe it."

"I don't know where to look first," Kate whispers in an awe-filled voice. "I could spend hours looking just at the painting on the ceiling and don't get me started on all the crests lining the walls."

The spacious ceremonial hall practically glitters as the bright wall sconces illuminate the dozens of gold-framed family crests which decorate three of the four walls. Sculptured friezes and an elaborate fresco painting draw the eye upwards. Red velvet drapes and cushions further emphasise the formal setting of the room.

I tap Kate's arm to bring her attention back to the floor level. "Why don't I show you to your seat so you can look your fill without blocking the entrance? Harry and I claimed a row of benches off to the side."

I barely get my friends settled before I see another familiar face standing in the doorway. Lavinia double-kisses my cheeks in greeting. She's joined by her husband, Filippo and his wife, and also Chiara. I'd hoped all three of Padua's prefects would be present for the ceremony, but I hadn't known for sure they were coming until now. Fortunately, there is plenty of space for them and their partners.

When the last of the arrivals take their seats, a member of the Italian delegation steps up to the lectern to begin the ceremony. As the speaker proceeds through the introductions and thanks, recognising all the various committees and contributors who worked to make this moment possible, I'm free to let my mind wander.

My first thought is for the man at my side. To think, only a year ago I was living alone in London, without a clue of what was in store for me. While I'd had plenty of ups and downs since my arrival in Oxford, the high points far outweighed the troughs. I found a home, a calling, a family, and love. Any of those things would be enough on their own. All together, they are a gift beyond my wildest hopes.

As I glance over to Padua's new prefects, I send up a silent request that they will find the same joy and fulfilment as I have. Much like me, they've had a rocky introduction to magic and the Eternals. But they've also seen how working together, across time and space, can bring answers and opportunities.

With that thought comes a stunning revelation. I'd always thought of our ability to see the Eternals as magic. However, as Filippo discovered, bringing the magical field into alignment with our own was a scientific effort. With the right tools and the key people in place, the process is easily replicated.

The true magic of Oxford, and now Padua, isn't the connection. It is the chance we have to gain knowledge and insights from the great minds who walked the same roads before us.

Dr Radcliffe's voice recalls my attention to the front of the room. She speaks of the long history between Oxford and Padua, one which I hadn't known about before. While the twinship is new, the connection between the two centres of knowledge spans centuries.

What happens next catches even me off-guard. While my mind was elsewhere, more Eternals had slipped into the great hall, adding their approval to the newfound relationship.

As Dr Radcliffe and the Vice Chancellor of Oxford exchange symbolic gifts with the Italian delegation, a pair of Eternals join them at the front of the room. Galileo Galilei and Thomas Linacre, representing Padua and Oxford respectively, shake hands and then share a brotherly embrace.

As if on cue, I notice Elena Cornaro Piscopia has claimed a seat in the far corner of the room. And in her lap, basking in some well-deserved stroking, sits a very familiar black-scaled wyvern. The people to her left and right don't seem at all concerned that a ghost and a cat are sitting between them. If I need any reassurance that Padua's magical connection is working as it should, this is it.

I'm even more grateful for the confirmation when I spy H straighten up, with a very determined expression on his scaly face. My concern ratchets up a notch when he leaps down to the floor and disappears from my view.

"Oh no," I murmur under my breath.

"What's wrong?" Edward asks, giving me a worried glance from the corner of his eye.

I shift in my seat, searching for a better angle. It's no use. With the tightly packed rows and people filling the audience. I can't see where he went. "H is up to something."

Edward's eyes grow large. It was too much to hope that we might make it through one ceremony without H causing some kind of trouble. Edward leans over to Harry, passing the message on down the line.

Harry and Kate display similar worries, but Mathilde practically rubs her hands together with glee. If the magic is working as it should, no one will notice his antics. Her display of confidence gives me a little hope, but not enough to entirely kibosh my nerves.

A sudden motion catches my eye. It's H, emerging from the edge of his aisle. He turns his head left and right and then makes a dash across the gap between the chairs. His small shape is hardly more than a moving shadow as he ducks under the row of speakers sitting at the front of the room.

I keep up with his movements by watching closely. First, a man stretches his legs out, clearing a path for H to continue. The woman beside him uncrosses and recrosses hers next. On down the line it goes, each presenter seemingly oblivious despite changing position to let him pass.

When he reaches the base of the window, I wonder whether he is coming our way. He isn't that far from us. Maybe all he wanted was to be closer to his family.

But then the sweeping red velvet drape trembles. I bite my lip to keep from gasping as I watch the heavy material shiver and shake.

"Is he crawling up the curtain?" Edward asks under his breath.

I can't speak. All I can do is nod a yes.

I trace the full length of the floor-to-ceiling curtain with my eyes, watching until I see a fang-filled black snout poke above the metal rod holding the top of the curtain in place. First one set of talons and then the other wrap around the bar. Without making a sound, H pulls himself up until he perches on top of the curtain rod.

He catches my eye and gives me a toothy smile. Petrified by thoughts of what might come next, I mouth the words, "Stay there!" and hope he can read my lips.

Talk about wishful thinking.

Instead of doing as I ask, he spreads his wings wide. His eyes and snout are firmly fixed on the display table at the front of the room, the one holding the gifts and documents used during the ceremony.

For the life of me, I can't imagine what he has planned.

Is H cheeky? Yes. Deliberately destructive? Never.

I cross my fingers and toes as he dives from his perch and swoops over the heads of the audience and speakers alike. He soars forward, his wings angled to keep him on his path. Lower and lower he goes, ever closer to the table.

Only at the last second do I notice that one candle in the candelabra has gone out.

H had obviously recognised this issue and decided to do something about it. With a single cough of flame, he relights the candle as he passes over it, and then lands right back into the lap of Elena Cornaro Piscopia.

Edward barely turns a laugh into a cough. The rest of our group is fit to be tied. Once again, as always, H has made an indelible mark on our ceremony.

Lucky for him, I wouldn't have it any other way.

When the ceremony is over, our responsibilities in Padua come to an end. In the historic courtyard of Palazzo Bo, I can see signs of the strengthening connection to the magic all around us. Already, Eternals mix and mingle with the students, faculty, and visitors who wander through the historic building.

For his part, H is having a ball of a time playing hide and seek with his new lion friends from nearby Caffè Pedrocchi. Thank goodness only those of us in the know can see the pride of lions prowling up the stairs and along the upper floors. If the twinkle in Filippo's eye is any clue, I suspect he'll ask one of the lions to take him for a ride before long.

Lavinia stops us outside the Palazzo before we can say

goodbye. "Hold that thought," she says, grinning widely. "Nonna has asked me to pass along an invitation to come to her house this evening. I know it's your last night in Padua, but do you think you'd have time to stop by?"

Kate takes a second to glance around the group before declaring we can't do better than that. "I can't think of any more appropriate way to wrap up our time in Padua than spending the evening with you, your family, and our new friends."

"Can I come, too, Livvie?" H asks after seeing the lions off.

Lavinia leans over and pats him on the head. "Absolutely, H. There will be a special bowl of extra-cheesy pasta with your name on it."

We split off into smaller groups, going our separate ways for a few hours of final touring around before we meet at Nonna's house. Kate and Harry declare their intention to shop for souvenirs. Mathilde and Trevor opt to visit the Specola. As for me and Edward, we decide to make the most of the warm afternoon sun with a leisurely walk through Padua's famous botanical garden.

The sun is barely visible above the horizon when we arrive at Nonna's house. Edward stands at my side as I push the buzzer. Harry and Kate are resplendent in new Italian dresses. Mathilde, Trevor, and H make sure to admire them. The sunset washes the sky in shades of yellow and red, but already the first stars twinkle above us. Nonna welcomes us into her home with open arms, embracing us and kissing our cheeks before letting us inside.

The warm interior and delicious smells wafting from the kitchen draw us deeper inside. Lavinia and her mother are waiting in the front room. Filippo arrives last, coming in on our heels. Lavinia's mum offers us all glasses of prosecco and then sends us through the house and into the back garden.

Outside, we find a long table for ten sitting underneath a

white canopy. Small torches provide plenty of light for us to see our way around without blocking our view of the starry sky.

As we chat and laugh, we enjoy little bites from the tray of hors d'oeuvres. H is delighted when Lavinia points him towards a bowl of cherry-sized mozzarella balls and paper-thin slices of prosciutto she'd set aside just for him.

Nonna is all smiles this evening, somehow seeming to stand straighter despite her stooped posture and age. When we finally take our seats around the table, I find out why.

"Before we eat, I want to take a moment to thank you all for your help in uncovering the truth of my sister's death. For nearly half a century, I've carried a weight on my shoulders, one which even I didn't understand. It was as though some part of me couldn't accept that her death was an accident." Nonna takes a breath and then continues, "When you found those threatening letters in Angelina's things, you opened my eyes to new possibilities. Today, Lavinia told me she was as certain as she could be that it was Angelina's dearest friend Rosa who was responsible for her death. As soon as she said those words, I felt a great peace settle over me."

Nonna's eyes sparkle with tears as her emotions get the better of her. Lavinia's mum steps in to speak for her. "You have my thanks as well. My mother seems ten years younger since she spoke with Lavinia. As for Angelina, for the first time in decades, I feel as though she is here with us, letting us know she is okay."

Nonna, once again in control, says her final words. "Tomorrow, I will visit Angelina's grave and tell her we know what happened to her."

"I bet you'll also give her an earful for keeping secrets from you," Lavinia pipes up, making us all laugh.

"That, too," Nonna agrees. "She and I will have a good chat, for as long as these old bones of mine will permit. Tonight, however, is for the living. This special dinner is my way of saying grazie tantissime. Please, eat as much as you can and stay as long as you like. It is my pleasure to have you as guests in my home."

Lavinia and her mum help the housekeeper carry dish after dish of food out to the table. Nonna had apparently decided we had to try every local delicacy, and enlisted the aid of her daughter and housekeeper in preparing mountains of food. Not that we complain. From squid ink risotto to sea bass to the more typical pasta choices, we try a bite of everything, arguing over our favourites and jostling for seconds.

I beg for an interlude to stretch my legs before dessert is served. Nonna shoos us away when we try to carry our plates and cutlery to the kitchen, refusing to let us do anything to help. Instead, she suggests we relax in the garden, and perhaps search the sky for familiar constellations.

I'm standing on my own when crunching leaves drag me from my sky-gazing. I expect to see Edward, but instead, it is Filippo who has sought me out.

"Ciao, Natalie," he says in greeting. He offers me a glass of dark liquid and explains it is an amaro.

"Cheers!" We clink our glasses together. I take a wary sip, and am relieved to find it tastes like liquorice. I glance behind him, back toward the table. "Are they serving dessert?"

"Not yet," he answers. He shuffles his feet for a moment and I clue in that he has something he wants to discuss. "I owe you a special thanks for not letting my stubbornness hold me back from being a part of Padua's future."

"You were determined to prove me wrong," I agree. "But don't worry, I didn't take it personally. You are a policeman, Filippo. Of course, you needed proof!"

Filippo chuckles at the truth in my words. "Yes, I did. But I might have discovered it sooner if I hadn't dug in my heels and refused to listen to you, Lavinia, and the others. I'm not sure I'll ever forget being dressed down by my childhood idol, Galileo."

"He was a man, just like you," I remind him. "Yes, his discoveries revolutionised the world as he knew it. But he was also a man of science and refused to accept things at face value. He was hard on you last night because you needed a firm hand to drag you into believing. From now on, I suspect you'll find your conversations go much easier."

"Let's hope so," Filippo murmurs before giving me a wink. His expression turns serious again, and he fumbles for words as he runs a hand through his hair.

"Is there something else?" I ask, prodding him.

He nods. "I understand I am your counterpart. Today, I got a glimpse of what you do in your role as Head of Ceremonies. Am I... err, that is... Do I have to plan events like that?"

He looks so terrified at the notion that I can't hold back a snort of laughter. "Part of me wants to say yes just so I can see your reaction. However, the real answer is no. You don't have to plan parties or organise events. A week ago, I thought it was part of the job. Now I know it is part of *my job*, but it isn't a prerequisite. You and I are caretakers for the people of our hometowns. I do my part by overseeing events. You will do yours in your own way — by keeping people safe and solving the crimes that happen."

Filippo sighs heavily, and his shoulders loosen in relief. "I can do that."

"You can, and you'll soon discover that the magic will give you an ace up your sleeve. I suggest you have a chat with Mathilde's boyfriend, Trevor. He's a detective in Oxford and is also learning how to make use of the Eternals to bring a quicker resolution to his investigations."

That gets Filippo's attention. "Really? I hadn't thought of that."

"You'll have to work with Lavinia and Chiara to expand the

magical borders around the town, but once you do, you'll have a very unique set of informants to help you along your way."

I leave Filippo to ponder that thought when Lavinia calls us back for dessert. Over bowls of creamy tiramisu with a rich coffee flavour, discussion turns to what is next in store for our little group.

"Nat is the busiest of all of us," Kate says, turning the conversation my way.

"No kidding! Now that term is starting, I've got my normal roster of events and ceremonies to plan on top of organising our wedding and finishing the house remodel."

"Don't mention it," Edward begs. "Every day a new bill arrives for us to settle. I don't begrudge us a pence of the money we're spending, but I think our Christmas gifts this year will have to be light fixtures and cans of paint."

"I hope you mean for each other and not for the rest of us," Harry chimes in. "Not that you don't have my sympathy. Rob and I weren't brave enough to attempt both a wedding and a remodel at the same time. I can well imagine it is hard on the pocketbook."

Lavinia's mum and nonna agree with Harry's sentiments and before long I'm passing around my phone to show pictures of what we've done so far. With Nonna's permission, Edward and I excuse ourselves so he can look at the Venetian glass chandelier in her dining room.

By the time we return, Kate and Mathilde have finished sharing information on their own plans. As I take a seat, Mathilde nudges Kate.

"Go ahead, Kate. You should at least see if she's interested."

"Interested in what?" I ask.

"No, it was just a silly thought. I'm sure you're too busy," Kate replies. However, neither Mathilde nor Harry is content to let her go quiet.

I wave my hand, telling her to get on with it.

Kate sighs, knowing she is beat. "A friend of mine owns a big country house in the Cotswolds. She mentioned she had an idea for a themed weekend, but she was having trouble finding someone who could organise it on such short notice. She was hoping to hold it near Christmas. But you've got so much going on already, Nat, that I didn't see any point in raising the idea."

Kate is one hundred per cent correct. I don't have either the time or the mental bandwidth to take on another project.

Not on my own, anyway.

But I can already envision doorways hung with sprigs of mistletoe and branches of ivy twisting up a staircase railing... bright red holly berries and the gleam of candlelight off Christmas bobbles.

"Oh no," I hear Kate grumble. "She's got that look in her eyes. Quick, Edward, bring her back to Earth."

"I'm hardly that foolish. I know better than anyone what happens to people who stand in Nat's way. If she wants to organise a last minute, Christmas-themed weekend, I'm not going to be the one to tell her she can't do it."

I give him a quick peck on the cheek as a reward for his reply. "Don't worry, darling. I'm sure our friends here will be happy to lend a hand. And you know, we could use the money..."

"Before you start your planning," Kate interjects, "I should probably tell you what theme she has in mind."

"It isn't a Christmas theme?"

"Not exactly," Kate answers. She's trying so hard not to laugh that she can hardly choke out the words. "It's a weekend getaway with an Agatha Christie-style murder mystery."

If Kate hopes that piece of news will discourage me, she's in for a surprise. Without batting an eye, I meet her gaze and offer this reply.

"If it's a party with a murder she wants, I'm more than qualified."

Stay tuned as Nat and her friends return in the next Oxford Keys Mystery: Homicide at Holly Manor, coming Winter 2022. Sign up for my newsletter to get notified when it is available.

Oxford and Padua - the real story

When I decided it was time for the Oxford crew to take a trip abroad, my first inclination was to send them to Venice. However, my husband had a different suggestion. On an afternoon walk, he looked at me and said, "You should send them to Padova."

At first, I brushed off his suggestion. My husband is from Padova, has generations of history in the town, and will argue until he is blue in the face that it is one of the best cities in the world.

However, as he went on to explain his rationale, I discovered his reasoning was sound. Padua and Oxford are indeed twin cities in real life, and he should know since he was part of the University of Oxford team that worked on the project.

Oxford and Padua have a centuries-long history of visits between scholars, fostering collaborations and inspiring discoveries. Thomas Linacre, whom I mentioned in the book, is one such example, but there are many others. It goes beyond the people. Oxford's Botanic Garden (featured in Sabotage at Somerset) is said to have been inspired by its counterpart in Padua.

You can find more information on Oxford's twin city relationship with Padua on the Oxford City Council website.

Although I built my idea on the basis of a true connection, I took great liberties with reality when writing this story. I did not interview my husband for any details of how the actual twinning process took place, nor do I know how they celebrated the event. Sometimes fiction is more fun than truth, and I didn't want to let pesky details get in the way of my final vision. If there is any overlap between fact and fiction, it is purely happenstance.

Homicide at Holly Manor

OXFORD KEY MYSTERIES - BOOK SEVEN

Nat's murder mystery weekend wasn't supposed to include a real dead body.

For event planner Natalie Payne, organising a murder mystery themed weekend getaway seemed like an easy way to make some extra money. But Nat's plans go awry when the wrong person is found dead.

Somewhere within the holly berry and mistletoe filled halls hides a murderer. Can Nat and her friends find out the truth, or will one of them be the next victim?

Find out in Winter 2022. Make sure you don't miss out by signing up for my newsletter at LynnMorrisonWriter.com.

Stakes and Spells

STAKES AND SPELLS MYSTERIES - BOOK ONE

If you like the Oxford Key Mysteries, check out my other paranormal cozy mystery series.

Every vampire knows better than to get involved with the witches.

But surely spying on one little ritual couldn't hurt, right? Wrong.

One minute I'm lurking behind a tombstone, the next a witch is dead and somehow I've inherited her magical powers!

With a dead body by my side and witch power in my veins, there's no way I won't get the blame. Especially once the Supernatural Bureau takes on the case.

Will a clever cat familiar, a witch with nothing to lose, and a grimoire of spells be enough to save my fangs from a future behind bars?

It'll take magic and a miracle to keep a certain werewolf Special Agent from sniffing out my hiding place before I can prove my innocence.

Grab Stakes and Spells now for free: Get it now on Amazon

Acknowledgments

Thanks as always to my editing team of Inga Kruse, Anne Radcliffe, and Ken Morrison. A big thanks to Brenda Chapman who bravely agreed to read an early version of the first half of the book and encouraged me to keep going.

My husband and mother-in-law graciously answered all my questions about Padua and its history. They've been around me long enough to know when I ask a random question, it is easier to just answer it. In my effort to get things right, I tapped into their knowledge as locals to fill in the gaps between what I could find online and in my own memories. Any mistakes are my own!

Emilie Yane Lopes continues to amaze me with the fantastic original cover designs for this series. Her incredible skill really makes my work shine.

I cannot express enough gratitude to everyone who has taken the time to drop me an email or comment on Facebook to let me know how much they enjoy this series. There were (and always will be) many days in which the doubts shout louder than my dreams. When that happens, knowing someone else cares about these characters as much as I do makes a world of difference.

Last, but never least, thanks to my children for putting up with a mother who lives in her own head. Thanks to my mom for letting me borrow my dad's time. And thanks to the cats for keeping me company as I write.

About the Author

Lynn Morrison lives in Oxford, England with her husband, two daughters and two cats. Originally from the US, she has also lived in Italy, France and the Netherlands. It's no surprise then that she loves to travel, with a never-ending wish list of destinations to visit. She is as passionate about reading as she is writing, and can almost always be found with a book in hand. You can find out more about her on her website LynnMorrisonWriter.com.

You can chat with her directly in her Facebook group - Lynn Morrison's Not a Book Club - where she talks about books, life and anything else that crosses her mind.

facebook.com/nomadmomdiary

twitter.com/nomadmomdiary

instagram.com/nomadmomdiary

bookbub.com/authors/lynn-morrison

goodreads.com/nomadmomdiary

Also by Lynn Morrison